WARNINGS IGNORED!

Don Ball
Fred Freitas

The Story of the Portland Gale of 1898

100th Anniversary Edition
PORTLAND GALE
November 27, 1898

"REMEMBER THE MAINE"
32 UNITED STATES OF AMERICA 32

SCITUATE, MA
NOVEMBER
27
1898
02066

The
Portland
Gale
Station

U.S. Life-Saving Station: North Scituate

This is an account of one of the South Shore's epic storms. It is a story of destruction, heroism and lives saved and lost.

Researched, written and published by Fred Freitas and Dave Ball.

ISBN: 0-9815720-6-5

Digitally reproduced in 2008 by:
Converpage - *Digital Reproductions*
23 Acorn Street, Scituate, MA 02066
www.converpage.com

Table of Contents

CHAPTER 1- PROLOGUE

CHAPTER 2- THE RAGTIME ERA--LIFE IN THE 1890'S

CHAPTER 3- FIRST WARNING! THE TEMPEST IS BORN!

CHAPTER 4- THE LIFESAVERS & THE SOUTH SHORE STATIONS

CHAPTER 5- NORTH SCITUATE & FOURTH CLIFF LIFE-SAVING STATIONS

CHAPTER 6- POINT ALLERTON, BRANT ROCK AND GURNET STATIONS

CHAPTER 7- ALERT DISREGARDED

CHAPTER 8- ANXIETY AND HEARTACHE: THE COLUMBIA & VARUNA

CHAPTER 9- BRAVERY AT BLACK ROCK

CHAPTER 10- DISASTERS ALONG THE SHORE

CHAPTER 11- RENDEZVOUS WITH DESTRUCTION: LOSS OF THE PORTLAND

CHAPTER 12- SCITUATE DEVASTATED!

CHAPTER 13- WRECK AND RUIN ON THE SOUTH SHORE

CHAPTER 14- THE AFTERMATH

CHAPTER 15- ONE HUNDRED YEARS LATER

CHAPTER 16- STEAMER PORTLAND FOUND!

Introduction

On November 26 and 27, 1898, a storm of epic proportions struck New England and wreaked havoc along the coastline, particularly the coast along the South Shore and Cape Cod. This year we commemorate the 100th anniversary of that great storm with this special 100th anniversary edition. Activities for this occasion include the placing of a plaque at the sight of the pilot boat Columbia's grounding in Sandhills, the renaming of the Sea Street bridge into Humarock after Frederick Stanley the keeper of the Fourth Cliff Life-Saving Station, and a special one day stamp cancellion at Scituate and Humarock Post Offices and the Maritime and Irish Mossing Museum. The special cancellation stamp was designed by Jake Donohue, a sixth grade student at Gates Intermediate School, while the five cachet envelopes were fashioned by Richard "Skip" Toomey and Stacey Hendrickson, who are both art teachers also at Gates Intermediate School.

As children we were brought up with tales of New England and her storms. Hurricanes, nor'easters, gales and the sagas that accompanied them became part of our learning -- on an equal footing with Math and English. Uncles and aunts regalled us with tales of courage, tragedy and human foolhardiness, so that to us, Portland was a ship long before it was a city.

Now as adults we have attempted to find out the whole story behind these childhood tales. From historical rooms to micro-film libraries -- from archives to cataloguer's vaults, we have searched for answers. In this pursuit we have had the assistance of many people, and we would like to take an opportunity to publically thank them.

In addition to all those who originally aided us in the research on this volume and who were listed in the 1995 edition, we would like to add and give recognition to Barbara Driscoll and Ross Sherbrooke from the Humane Society of the Commonwealth of Massachusetts for their aid and support of this project. To John Galluzzo, education director and historian at Hull Life-Saving Museum, thank you for your assistance. To Mr. Robert McNamara, owner of McNamara-Sparrell Funeral Homes, for providing us with records relating to those who lost their lives in Scituate due to the storm - thank you. To all our friends at the Scituate Historical Society, without you this book would not have been possible. To our wives, Jean and Joanne, whose faithful, persistent, and encouraging support and assistance these many months is truly appreciated. Lastly to you the reader, thank you for your interest in local history, for as Stephen Spender said, "history is the ship carrying living memories to the future." -- so again welcome aboard!!

CHAPTER 1
Prologue

"Ask me no more: thy fate and mine are sealed. . ." Tennyson

BOSTON

"Wait, please wait!" Jes Smith yelled as the gate was closed and the steward of the Portland prepared for departure. As the steward turned, Jes continued, "My ship has just arrived from Denmark, and my family and I have rushed so that we could make this sailing."

The steward smiled and replied, "If you had arrived a few seconds later, it would have been too late. Here, let me help you!" He helped Jes, his wife and two young sons on board in the gathering darkness.

Before several minutes more had passed, the Portland had slowly pulled away from India Wharf in Boston and steamed into the darkness.

Suddenly a running figure appeared out of the dark. Clutching baggage and puffing from the exertion, a red-faced man emotionally chastised himself. "Leonard Dora, you fool!" he rebuked. "You had to have just one more drink. You had to have just a little more conversation with your friend. Oh, right! You'd keep track of the time. Why they'll hold the ship, they said they would you so boldly boasted! But not while you waste time in a bar!!" As the darkness gradually swallowed the Portland, a snowflake floated ominously down alighting gently. Dora angrily turned away wondering where he would stay for the night. As he walked down the street, he noticed the snow.

SCITUATE

A slicker-covered figure made his way up the stairs of the cottage. Reaching the door he firmly knocked. "Coming," came the reply. The door slowly opened. "Yes, what can I do for you," a middle-aged man asked the figure.

"I'm surfman Tobin from the North Scituate Life-Saving Station. We are warning residents that a severe storm is approaching, and that for your own safety you should leave and take shelter inland."

"Thank you for the warning, but I'm sure my wife and I are perfectly safe."

"I know the weather looks fine," replied Tobin, "but here in the Sandhills, cottages will be in peril if the storm is severe."

"Mrs. Wilbur and I have taken precautions," Mr. Wilbur stated. "We have left the horse harnessed to the buggy just in case. Thank you again for your concern Surfman Tobin. Good night."

Leonard Dora, Jes Smith and his family, Mr. and Mrs. Wilbur and thousands of other New Englanders' fates would be irrevocably sealed when a storm of intense magnitude intervened the night of November 26-27, 1898. New England would never be the same again.

CHAPTER 2

The Ragtime Era--Life in the 1890s

"This village (Scituate) is noted for its quaintness, its old-time streets and drives, and its fine sea coast; here we find an abandoned lighthouse." E. G. Perry May, 1898

"Get your **Boston Post** here, only 1 cent!"

"See the Little Magnet, Lottie Gilson, plus 20 Blue Ribbon Beauties perform. They're waiting for you at the **Old Howard**. Just 25 cents for a reserved seat! Come one! Come all!"

"Take the palatial steamer **Portland** for a day's excursion at sea. Leaving India Wharf every evening at 7 p.m. The fare is $1.00. Hurry, don't wait!"

What was life in the 1890s like? Myths of history persist, and we must separate myth from reality. The reality is we have little in common with these distant ancestors. Our lives have been more directly influenced by more recent family and events, not far distant ones.

Change was the catch word in the 1890s. It was during this era that modern America emerged on the world stage. More than half the United States still earned a living on the farm, and communities south of Boston were no exception. This would soon change! The industrial revolution altered life in all areas: work, transportation, communication, living in general. Bustling cities attracted more and more Americans to them. This was not all. Americans were transformed by new modes of travel: railroads, steamships, streetcars and trolleys.

Trolley at Nantasket Photo courtesy of Richard Cleverly

A new word began to creep into Americans' vocabulary-- leisure. New ways of working and

of traveling also generated new ways to play. Bicycles, amusement parks, baseball,and beach-going were added to, or replaced, the front porch and church as free time activities. Seemingly there didn't appear to be anything holding people back from doing what they wanted.

The Chutes at Nantasket -- an early water ride. Photo courtesy of Richard Cleverly.

Growth, progress, and change became the notes of the music heralding a new century. It was an age of promise, an age of bright hope, and a time to be proud and happy to be an American.

In trying to picture what Scituate and the South Shore were like in 1898, it is necessary to put aside the technological advantages that today we take for granted. Communication then was very primitive. While some had phone service, it was far from being universal. Telegraph messages were the most important link between regions of the country. The dependability of these messages was contingent on many unreliable conditions, not the least of which, was weather.

The highway then most used was not one of information, but one composed of either water, iron, or dirt. A person living then might use any one of these highways for travel, or he might use all three. All of these modes of transportation could be beset by unexpected delays. People, therefore, tended to live in isolated conditions.

The people who resided along the coast from Hull to Duxbury were substantially fewer in number than today. In 1898 the total population for Hull, Cohasset, Scituate, Marshfield and Duxbury was less than half Scituate's present population of just over 18,000. With less people distributed over a land area equal to today, this isolation was heightened. Americans did not know what was happening in other parts of the United States, or even in other towns around them. Those who lived in Scituate associated more with their particular village than with the town as a whole. Scituate Center, North Scituate, Minot, Egypt, Sandhills, Cedar Point, The Harbor, Greenbush, the West End, and Humarock were the villages.

p. 4

Rare 1869 photo of Hull looking north.

Photo from early 1890's at Cedar Point, Scituate.

The Cliff House, Minot Beach, No. Scituate, Mass.

The Scituate of 1898 was different from today in other ways. Farm Neck, the land north of Musquashicut Pond, in the early 1800s was the location of several large farms, but by the 1890s it housed several hotels for the beach-going public. This reflected the increased awareness of leisure and a changing attitude toward its pursuit. The Minot, The Rockland, The Cliff House, and the Mitchell House were several well-known establishments. Hotels, however, were not limited to North Scituate. The Grandview and Hatherly Inn were located in the Sandhills/ Barker Farm area while the Stanley House and Carson Inn were in the Harbor. The palatial Humarock Hotel anchored Scituate's southern boundary. These beach front hotels were located not just in Scituate, but all along the South Shore. The Hotel Nantasket in Hull and The Brant Rock Hotel in Marshfield are just two of many other examples. Visitors to these hotels would travel by horse-drawn buggies or barges from the railroad or trolley stations to them.

One additional difference was that Humarock was joined to the Third Cliff by a narrow shingle barrier beach, and this beach had a gravel road across it. This was one means of leaving Humarock. The other was by bridge. This bridge across the North River had been constructed by the Fourth Cliff Land Company, a company whose purpose was "to manage and improve the land at their discretion, with the most unlimited power, and to mortgage or sell . . . the land". In 1884 the town gave the Fourth Cliff Land Company a quitclaim deed to all the land or Hummocks below Fourth Cliff between the North River and the ocean to low water mark.

Another difference in life then involved farming since farming during the 1890s was the occupation of over fifty percent of all Americans. Many South Shore farms sold their produce to the numerous seasonal hotels, or took it to Boston by horse and wagon -- an eight hour trip. Farmers worked long hours every day, seven days a week, and fifty-two weeks a year. Some farmers preferred to sell their produce in the city, so once the crop was harvested it was time for the trip there. They would drive their horse-drawn wagons loaded with goods to Boston. There the produce was sold to wholesalers right off the wagon.

There were several means of travel from the South Shore to Boston. You could take the train, make the long journey by horse, or go by boat. Travel by horse was the predominant means of movement in the late nineteenth century, and because of this, many associated industries and occupations developed that reflected the horse's importance. Blacksmiths, wheelwrights, livery stables, harness makers, painters of the carriages, shays, pungs, etc. were needed. The horses had to eat, so there were hay and grain suppliers as well. Horse-drawn wagons brought meat, vegetables and fruit, ice, coal, wood, and other goods directly to homes. Horses moved furniture, students, travelers, caskets, fire engines, boats, houses and road-watering machines within town.

The railroad on the South Shore was owned and operated by the New York, New Haven & Hartford Railroad Company. Railroad spurs ran from Braintree to Plymouth and an additional line from Braintree through Weymouth south through Hingham, Cohasset, Scituate, Marshfield and Duxbury before it merged with another line at Kingston. Scituate had four stations located within its borders -- North Scituate, Egypt, Scituate Center and Greenbush. Trolleys and electric trains also serviced parts of the South Shore. An electric train, in addition to the steam-powered train that ran from Nantasket Junction to Nantasket to Pemberton, ran from Nantasket Junction (The present location of Hingham Lumber) to Pemberton.

Part of this route was electrified by a third rail. So popular was this electric car route that from 1897 on, it would carry one million people a season! Most of these summer travelers loved the open platform coaches. The ladies who dressed in white, frilly attire hated the dirty steam-powered engines of the railroad, but flocked to the airy electric cars. And where the ladies went, the men would soon follow. Later third rails were added to Braintree and to Cohasset.

Steamship lines also serviced people from the South Shore going to Boston and vice-versa. The Hingham Hull & Downer Steamboat Co. delivered passengers from Boston to Pemberton, Nantasket and ended at Hingham Harbor.

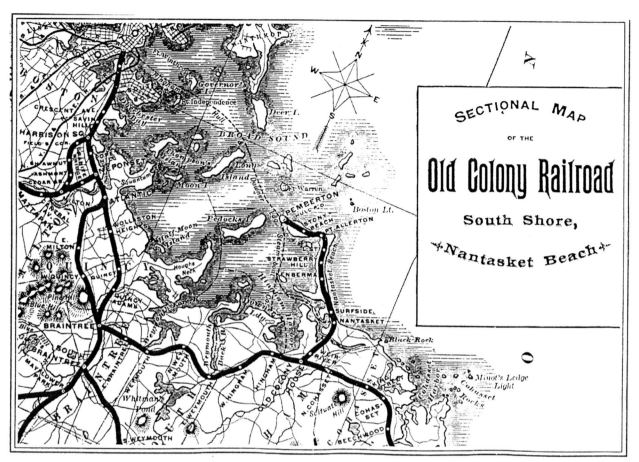

Map courtesy of Bob Chessia.

Train station at North Scituate.

If you lived in Scituate, your many occupational choices included: farmer, fisherman, ship captain, coastal trader, surfman, blacksmith, or Irish mosser. If you were a fisherman, your fish were probably sold at Bonney's Market in the Harbor. Bonney's also sold lobsters, coal and hay among other things. People purchased their lumber at the George F. Welch Company while others could have bowled or played pool at James Ward's alley.

For the romantic, a rented horse and buggy from George Brown's stable (only one of many) provided the means for an enjoyable afternoon excursion.

During the summer months ice cream could be purchased at Stenbeck's store, which today is the ticket entrance to Scituate Harbor theaters, or at Mrs. Lucy Wade's Ice Cream Parlor in North Scituate. They were the Wilbur's of 1898! Mrs. Wade also offered to do laundry work for families and hotels with satisfaction given.

Everything from pins to rubber boots was available at Charlie Frye's store, which was the only business on the west side of Front Street. The rest of the west side of Front Street was occupied by homes and stately elms.

If your needs ran to Chicago Beef, then you went to G. T. Otis' store near the train depot (near the Central Fire Station). Otis's cart also made daily trips throughout town for those unable to come to the store. Townspeople were advised by an ad from that period, "to talk to the driver for he'll give you the best prices and no lies." If you needed a real estate and insurance agent, Frederic T. Bailey, who was located opposite the depot in North Scituate, filled the bill.

In Greenbush a person brought household tools to be repaired at Clapp's Blacksmith Shop, then purchased ice at the Clapp's ice-house. The Clapp's grist mill was there, too, if it was needed. The Clapp family was one of the most prominent families in Greenbush. They trace their line back unbroken to Roger Clap (1609), who settled in Dorchester around June of 1630.[1] T. F. Kane's motto for his store was "Best Quality, Lowest Prices."

Looking east from the 3A intersection at Old Oaken Bucket Pond in Greenbush. Note the Eaton Hotel on the hill. Today sand from this hill is used as a cover at the landfill. Photo courtesy of Dorothy Langley.

---

[1] The Clapp family history is documented in a book by Dorothy (Clapp) Langley titled The Clapp Family, 1866-1986.

Front Street Scituate Harbor

p. 10

A person who needed to send or receive a telegraph went to Richardson's Pharmacy in the Harbor for this purpose. While there you might consider picking up Proprietor Richardson's

Turner's store on wheels.

unexcelled cough and lung remedies and any veterinary medicines needed for the farm.

Roland Turner's store on wheels, one of many such traveling stores, supplied goods to all sections of the town, particularly isolated farms, for over fifty years. His wagon was loaded with all manner of dry goods, cottons, boots, shoes, and hundreds of useful articles. He was also Treasurer and Collector for Scituate, so he combined official and private business by visiting practically everyone in Scituate over the years. Grocery stores provided many other household goods for the customers needs. Henry Ellm's store on Front Street in the harbor was just one example.

If you were of school age and lived in the western part of Scituate, you attended the new Hatherly School, which was located on the east side of Country Way near the corner of Hollett

Union School at First Parish and Stockbridge (Union Street then) Road - Scituate, Massachusetts 1898.

Street. It had opened on January 1, 1897. Transportation to and from school for those who needed it was by horse-drawn barge. The School Calendar for 1899 had 3 terms: Winter (Jan. 2 to Mar. 24), Spring (April 3 to June 23) and Fall (Sept. 5 to Dec. 22). The holidays included one day for the Marshfield Fair!

In their report to the citizens of the town in 1898 the School Committee noted, "The general progress of the schools has been seldom if ever more satisfactory." Later they mentioned salaries, " In the early part of the year it seemed advisable to increase the salaries of some of our teachers, which the Committee felt they do under the present appropriation; consequently the High School asistant received an addition of $50, making her salary $500 per year. The salary of the East Grammar principal was raised to the same amount; three primary teachers were given one dollar per week, and five others fifty cents per week additional. We hope another year to give all primary teachers the same." The High School graduating exercises were held at the Town Hall on Friday, June 24. Mr. Joy Gannett, Jr. of the School Committee handed out 14 diplomas. The large crowd enjoyed the varied and interesting program.

WHAT'S THE MATTER WITH KIDS AND PARENTS TODAY?

REPORT OF THE TRUANT OFFICER.

I have often hinted, more or less strongly, in my reports as Superintendent of Schools, that I believed parents were largely responsible for the unnecessary absences of their children. I do not suppose that I have investigated one-tenth part of the absences which have occurred during the past year : Neither do I presume that I have known of one-half of the cases of actual truancy, which have existed, but the facts below speak for themselves and go to show how far amiss my suppositions in regard to the attitude of parents have been.

The following is the report on truancy :--

Absent without sufficient reason,	15
Number of actual truants,	12
Number of cases investigated	27

Respectfully submitted.

EDGAR L. WILLARD

Truant Officer,

December 31st, 1898

Life all over the South Shore was similar to life in Scituate.

Two different forms of entertainment at Hull. Photos courtesy of Richard Cleverly.

CHAPTER 3

First Warning! The Tempest Is Born!

"The tempest was terrible and separated me from my (other) vessels that night,

putting every one of them in desperate straits, with nothing to look forward to

but death."   Christopher Columbus

𝔄 record-breaking 𝔑ovember blizzard swept over a greater portion of 𝔑ew 𝔈ngland yesterday and last night, completely demoralizing traffic of every description, and wellnigh paralyzing telegraphic and telephonic communications, while the northeast gale coming on a high course of tides, drove the sea far beyond its usual limits and made a mark along shore only exceeded by the memorable hurricane of 1851.
𝔅oston 𝔇aily 𝔄dvertiser 𝔑ovember 28, 1898

Modern meteorology was in its infancy in the late 1800s. While there was a good understanding of high and low pressure systems and their influence on the weather, other factors were not. Aspects such as fronts, upperlevel winds, and the jet stream would not be discovered until the 20th century.

The United States Army Signal Corp began providing weather data in 1872. Weather reports were disseminated to marine, railroad and commercial interests via telegraph, but the general public was forced to rely on newspaper reports for their daily weather information. Thus even though weather information was dispersed mainly by only one widereaching medium, the telegraph, it was still quite adequate for those with the greatest need for information. The Monthly Weather Review of November, 1898, provides detailed information of how and where this storm developed and the official warnings issued.

During the early part of November, 1898, several noteworthy storm systems had migrated across the United States and into the Great Lakes region. However, these storm systems had not severely affected New England. As the last of these storm systems moved into Canada on November 23, the stage was readied for the infamous gale of November 26 and 27.

On November 24 a cold front had swept south to the Gulf of Mexico and south Atlantic coasts and probably stalled, triggering a storm off the southeast coast of the United States. As that disturbance was becoming organized, a storm was plunging east-south-east toward the mid-Atlantic coastline. Alarmed these two lows would merge into a dangerous storm, the U.S. Weather Bureau issued the following advisories for east coast interests at 10:30 a.m. on November 26. "Storm central near Detroit moving east. East to northeast gales with heavy snow to-night. Wind will shift to west and northwest with much colder temperatures Sunday." Additionally a special warning was telegraphed to all Weather Bureau offices in New York and New England. "Heavy snow indicated for New York and New England to-night. Notify railroad and transportation interests." The fact these warnings were issued so early in the day when weather conditions were

still tranquil in New England is significant as will be seen in the next chapters.

The forecasters concern was soon confirmed. By noon the Detroit low had raced to Pittsburg, Pa. and the coastal low had deepened rapidly and moved north to Cape Hatteras, N.C., a breeding ground for such storms. By 3 p.m. the lows had merged off Norfolk, Va. and begun the trek north -- destination New England! Even now though the public was unaware of the approaching disaster, for although the sky was now cloudy, the wind and snow were still several hours away.

Log entries by keepers all along the South Shore and the Cape show barometer readings quite high at the beginning of the day and then falling as the day advanced, but not so precipitously to cause undo alarm. One omen was certainly not sufficient warrant extra precautions be taken by the keepers, especially when other indicators of a major storm had not yet developed.

Snow began to fall in Boston at 7:37 p.m., lightly at first, but with each passing hour, the intensity of the snowfall and wind grew. Two hours later even seasoned mariners were stunned by the increasing violence of the storm. Captains at Boston and other major ports, who earlier in the day had heeded their own senses or the advice of the Weather Bureau, were now glad they had remained in port. In the early evening masters on scores of vessels off the Cape and Islands realized they were in for a bad blow and scrambled for the nearest port.

As the awful night wore on conditions became steadily worse. Everyone was now aware of what the forecasters had predicted 12 hours earlier. Only the oldest residents of the South Shore and Cape Cod who could recall the gale of April, 1851 that toppled Minot's Light had ever experienced an assault on the ears equal to the wind they now heard. At sea, hundreds of vessels caught in the grips of the increasing gale reefed sails and bucked monstrous seas. On shore conditions became increasingly savage at the breaking of the new day -- Sunday. Some residents certainly must have believed they were in the grips of an out of control hurricane. Today we know it was not a hurricane at all, but rather a powerful gale of nearly unprecedented strength.[2] The storm continued to rage during the morning of the 27th, but at Chatham and Barnstable on Cape Cod, the skies cleared and wind slackened briefly at 9:30 a.m. Fifteen minutes later the clouds and wind returned. Observers on the Cape noticed that many of the largest trees in that area were wrenched from the ground in the next half hour. The briefly clearing skies point to the fact that the center of the storm passed diagonally across the Cape at that time and moved into Massachusetts Bay on its way northeast. The fact the storm had a clear eye indicates the tremendous strength of the low. It was not until late in the day on Sunday that conditions started to moderate.

J.W. Smith, Boston Weather Bureau observer:

November 26. "Clear morning, but weather clouded up as the day advanced, and snow began to fall at 7:37 p.m., becoming heavy after 9:30 p.m. Light west winds until noon, then shifted to easterly and northeasterly at 2:45 p.m., and slowly increasing in force during the afternoon and

---

2 The 1898 and the 1978 storms were similar, but the 1978 one was more powerful and produced even higher winds and tides.

evening -- Much inquiry for information from transportation, shipping, railroad, and other interests.

November 27. "The storm increased greatly in severity during the night, becoming one of the most severe for years. From 3:00 a.m. to 1 p.m. the hourly wind velocity ranged from 40 to 50 miles, with a maximum velocity of 60 miles at 11:00 a.m. and an extreme velocity of 72 miles per hour at 11:02 a.m."

Wind speeds recorded at Boston were lower than elsewhere along the South Shore and the Cape for two reasons. The storm was compact yet powerful and therefore locations south of the city were closer to the storm center. Additionally, the Boston office of the Weather Bureau was located directly in the city and therefore some distance from the waterfront.

This storm produced New England's worst maritime disaster ever with the loss of the steamer Portland and well over 100 vessels sunk or irreparably damaged--a dubious record never to be matched again.

Along the Massachusetts coast cottages, wharves and other infrastructure were destroyed, and in places the contour of the coastline itself was forever changed. Inland thousands of trees were blown down leaving South Shore towns scarred for decades.

Some researchers have attempted to demonstrate a correlation between major East Coast storms and the full or new moon phases. We do point out that this storm occurred at full moon. Also compounding coastal damage was the timing of high tide with the height of the tempest coinciding with high tide at 10:30 a.m. November 27.

(a) 8 a. m.

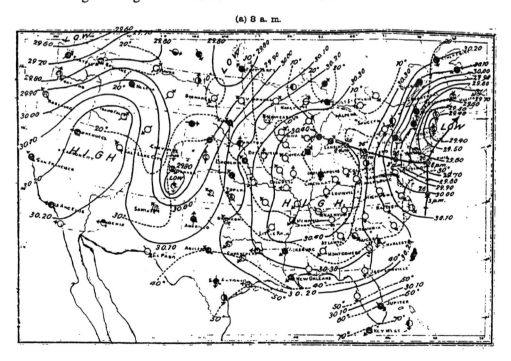

Weather Bureau Map
November 27 -- 8 a.m.
Note low off the
New England Coast. The
odd appearance of this map
is because no fronts
are shown.

CHAPTER 4
Life-savers and The South Shore Stations

"Greater love hath no man than this that a man lay down his life for his friends."
Epitath on the gravestone of Joshua James, keeper of the Point Allerton Life-Saving Station, Hull, and this
country's greatest life-saver.

The hunched figure of a man leaned into the sand-whipped wind as he trudged his way down the desolate beach. The sand, which stung his face and hands, managed to invade his slicker and uncomfortably form a thin layer of grit over his body. As he made his way along the beach, he constantly peered seaward observing everything possible. He paused and tried to listen over the thunderous roar of the storm-tossed water. Leaning down he picked up a piece of flotsam that had been left by a rapidly receding wave. His body tensed and he glanced quickly around. Picking up more objects he stared intently toward the sea. With night vision heightened by years of experience, he picked out the skeletal image of ship caught on the ledge and battered by mountainous waves. Quickly he removed a tube-like object from his pocket. He struck the top, and a brilliant reddish white light shone forth. This was the signal that help was on the way. This scene was one that would be repeated throughout the late nineteenth and early twentieth centuries. The man was a surfman from the United States Life-Saving Service and this was his job.

A BRIEF HISTORICAL SKETCH OF EARLY LIFE-SAVING EFFORTS

As early as the late 1700s it was obvious a need existed to provide assistance to the crews of ships wrecked on the Massachusetts coast. Several wealthy concerned citizens organized the Humane Society of the Commonwealth of Massachusetts in 1785 to meet this need. In 1792 six huts of refuge were built, and in 1807 the society constructed the first station fitted with a lifeboat on the coast at Cohasset. By 1845 there were 18 stations located at critical points along the most desolate and dangerous sections of the coast. The stations were manned by volunteers, who came only when needed, and were equipped with boats and line throwing guns. The Humane Society continued to maintain stations into the first part of this century. The Society was the precursor to the United States Life Saving

p. 17

States Life Saving Service, which eventually became the United States Coast Guard in 1915.

photo courtesy of Richard Cleverly

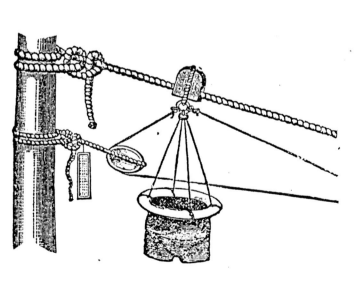

p. 18

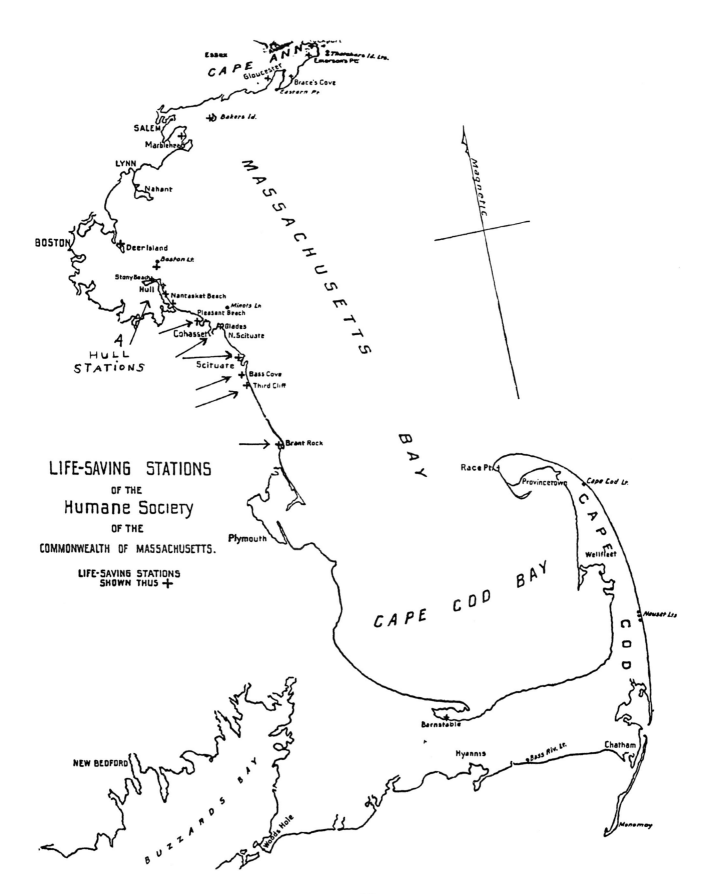

LIFE-SAVING STATIONS
OF THE
Humane Society
OF THE
COMMONWEALTH OF MASSACHUSETTS.

LIFE-SAVING STATIONS
SHOWN THUS +

Between 1847 and 1871 the United States Congress appropriated monies sporadically for the construction and manning of Life-Saving stations. In 1854 there were 137 stations located at various places along the U.S. coast. However, the effort lacked real commitment on the part of the Federal government. Some stations did have paid crews, but they were poorly trained and the equipment was badly maintained.

During the winter of 1870-71 a series of fatal shipwrecks occurred along the Atlantic coast. These losses clearly pointed out the fact the coast was not properly protected and that the service was totally inefficient. A complete overhaul was long overdue.

In 1871 Congress appropriated $200,000 to establish a reliable service. Sumner Kimball, the head of the Revenue Marine Service, ordered an inspection of all existing stations. The investigator's report was shocking. Most of the facilities were in ruins, the equipment stolen or in unusable condition, and the existing crews undisciplined. With the new infusion of money, the Unites States Life-Saving Service fired many of the crews, employed only the most skilled surfmen and station keepers and constructed a number of new stations.

These new stations were plain houses mostly measuring 42' by 18' of two stories and four to 5 rooms.[3] One room below was used by the crew as a mess room, the other room housed the boats and equipment for rescues. One of the upper rooms housed the sleeping quarters and the other was for storage.

Every station had a lookout or observatory where life-savers would keep careful track of all coastal shipping. So that ships at sea would be able to easily recognize the stations, the roofs were usually painted dark red. As an additional aid to ships, a flagpole about sixty feet in height was erected nearby. Signal flags were displayed on the pole using the International Code. The use of these flags allowed ships to communicate with the stations to establish latitude and longitude or render assistance if needed.

Stations were manned from August 1 until June 1 of the next year, the keeper was on duty year round.

---

[3] There were several Life-Saving house designs, so there was some variety among stations.

Every station had 2 surf-boats, boat carriages , 2 sets of breeches-buoy apparatus, carts for transportation of this apparatus, a life car, life preservers, Coston signals and signal rockets. Also supplied were signal flags of International and General Signal Code, wooden medicine kit with contents, patrol lanterns, barometer, thermometer, patrol clocks, household furniture for the crew and rescued people, fuel, oil, tools, and the necessary books, charts and stationery.

North Scituate Life-Saving Station

The construction dates for the stations on the South Shore were:

Hull Life-Saving Station: 1889
North Scituate Life-Saving Station: 1886
Fourth Cliff Life-Saving Station: 1879
Brant Rock Life-Saving Station: 1892
Gurnet Life-Saving Station: 1891

All stations were normally manned by six surfmen and a keeper. Each surfman was assigned a number from one to seven to designate his order of senority and experience. With a surfman's pay of less than $50 per month, the long walk of each patrol, and the always present danger, it is understandable why only the most dedicated were interested in the job.

Hull Life-Saving Station

When the weather was good, four-hour patrols north and south of the station were conducted

at night commencing at sunset and terminating at sunrise. If inclement weather dictated, daytime patrols were also run. Some foot patrols were five miles in length and had to be conducted during all types of weather. It was all the more necessary to operate the patrols when weather conditions were extremely foul.

The patrol route from each station was mapped out. These routes were for night patrols, or day patrols in foggy or thick weather. When a patrolman met his fellow surfman from the adjoining station, they would exchange checks. If a surfman failed to show, then after a reasonable wait, the patrolman would continue on until he either met his fellow surfman or arrived at the next station to determine the cause of failure to meet. In stations where there was no overlap in patrol routes, a surfman carried a time-clock. At the end of his patrol route was a key post. Upon reaching this key post, the surfman punched his clock.

The surfmen rotated liberty from the station and the keeper carefully entered in the logs who was absent, the reason and the time of departure and arrival back at the station. One surfman was assigned the day watch. This surfman constantly scanned the horizon for passing vessels and carefully recorded the number of barks, brigs, schooners and sloops he saw pass by the station.

The keeper was in total charge of the station's operation. He handled all issues related to personnel, planned and oversaw the daily activities, and recorded all activities relating to his station including work accomplished and weather conditions every six hours.

A weekly routine was established. The week for a station began at midnight on Sunday with different procedures established for each day of the week:

Monday members of the crew put the station in order.

Tuesday, weather permitting, training drills for launching and landing the surfboat were practiced.

Wednesday the crew practiced the International and General Code of Signals.

Thursday, the men drilled using the breeches buoy and beach apparatus.

Friday, drills for resuscitating drowned victims were practiced.

Saturday was wash day, and **Sunday** was devoted to religious observances.

All of the above were done with the sole purpose of being ready to save lives!

Mass. Humane crews worked closely with the Life-Saving Service crews.

photo courtesy of Richard Cleverly

LIFE-SAVING DISTRICTS AND STATIONS IN THE UNITED STATES.

SECOND DISTRICT.

COAST OF MASSACHUSETTS.

Salisbury Beach........	Mass....	½ mile south of State line.........................	42 51 40	70 49 00
Newburyport........ ..	Mass....	North end of Plum Island, mouth of Merrimac River.	42 48 30	70 49 00
Plum Island..........	Mass....	On Plum Island, 2½ miles from south end.......	42 44 00	70 47 15
Straitsmouth b........	Mass....	½ mile west of Straitsmouth light..............	42 39 30	70 36 00
Gloucester.......... .	Mass....	Old House cove, westerly side of harbor, 1½ miles from town.	42 35 30 *	70 41 10
Nahant.............. .	Mass....	On the neck, close to Nahant..................	42 25 45	70 56 00
City Point...........	Mass....	Floating station in Dorchester Bay, Boston Harbor.		
Point Allerton........	Mass.. .	1 mile west of Point Allerton..................	42 18 20	70 54 00
North Scituate........	Mass....	2¼ miles south of Minots Ledge light..........	42 14 00	70 45 30
Fourth Cliff..........	Mass....	South end of Fourth Cliff, Scituate.............	42 09 30	70 42 10
Brant Rock..........	Mass.. .	On Green Harbor Point.......................	42 05 30	70 38 40
Gurnet..............	Mass ..	4½ miles northeast of Plymouth................	42 00 10	70 36 10
Manomet Point........	Mass ...	6½ miles southeast of Plymouth................	41 55 30	70 32 40
Wood End...........	Mass....	½ mile east of light..........................	42 01 15	70 11 30
Race Point..........	Mass....	1½ miles northeast of Race Point light.........	42 04 45	70 13 15
Peaked Hill Bars.......	Mass .	2¼ miles northeast of Provincetown............	42 04 40	70 09 50

a Obtained from latest Coast Survey charts.   b Formerly Davis Neck.

p. 23

CHAPTER 5

COUNTDOWN TO DEATH AND DISASTER

NORTH SCITUATE & FOURTH CLIFF LIFE-SAVING STATIONS NOVEMBER 26

" The method of selecting the life-saving crews has resulted in securing the most skillful and fearless surfmen, whose gallant deeds of heroism have made them famous throughout the land." J.W. Dalton

---

NORTH SCITUATE

George H. Brown had been keeper of the North Scituate station since December 15, 1886. Although he had dealt with several noteable storms since taking command, nothing would compare with what he and his surfmen were to face the following day.

Brown had observed the prior day that the seas had been rather rough, but as this day broke, the ocean was smooth and the skies were clear. A light wind was blowing from the northwest. He noted at dawn that the skies were clear. A light wind was blowing from the northwest. He wrote at dawn that it was 19° and the barometer was rather high and steady and the skies clear -- all the ingredients for a fair cold day-- hopefully an uneventful Saturday. The surfmen on duty this day would be: Jeremiah McCarthy, John E. Murphy, Richard W. Tobin, Edmund Landers, John Curran and Edward Ward. It was John Curran's turn to go on day leave for a few hours. He left in the morning to return home and arrived back at the station at 4 p.m.

The house was swept, all the brick and iron work cleaned and the house was ventilated for several hours. Coal and oil for lighting were expensive and the government expected Brown to produce a close accounting for these fuels on this day. Brown reported burning 150 lbs. of coal for cooking and heating and 3 qts. of oil for the lanterns.

All stations were interconnected by telephone. What storm warnings they received is unknown, for there was no place in their daily logs to enter such information. However, they may have been notified of the approaching foul weather.

All seemed normal as the day wore on except by noon the sky had clouded over and the barometer had fallen, but only slightly-- a possible warning that maybe there would be some work later that night. By sunset 15 schooners, 12 steamers and 2 sloops had passed the station.

FOURTH CLIFF

Guarding Scituate's southernmost border and located on the south side of the fourth cliff was Scituate's second Life-Saving station, the Fourth Cliff Station. It was opened on December 7, 1879 and continued operating into this century as both a Life-Saving Station and a Coast Guard Station. It lay just under the big bluff of that name and was very remote. The station had a seven

man crew and a 25 foot life boat. The keeper of the station was Fred Stanley. He had been appointed surfman at this station shortly after it opened. Nine months later Stanley was appointed keeper, a position he held until his retirement. "Cap" was thought highly of by the men who served under him. He was of medium height and compactly built. He was calm and firm by nature-- a no nonsense man. He was married and lived on the Third Cliff.

The northern patrol route for the Fourth Cliff station was across the gravel road on the shingle beach. Surfmen walked along the edge of the beach from the Fourth Cliff to the First Cliff. The mouth of river was located about 2 to 3 miles south of the Fourth Cliff near present day Rexhame Beach, Marshfield. This was the southerly patrol of the Fourth Cliff Station. From the Life-Saving station to the Hotel Humarock was a distance of about one and half miles over exposed low-lying sand dunes. In inclement weather this stretch of beach left the patrolling surfmen in a vulnerable position to be buffeted by wind, sand, salt spray and water. A newpaper article in 1890 described this stretch of beach as an arid stretch of desert sand backed by beach stones for more than two miles. The only interruption was the palatial Hotel Humarock.

Rare photo of the beach connecting Third and Fourth Cliffs before the storm. Photo courtesy of Cynthia Krusell.

The week ended at midnight on Saturday November 26, 1898. The wind was light and from the northwest; it was clear and a strong surf was running. Richard Wherity, number 5 surfman, and J. Flynn, surfman number 2, were on the north and south midnight patrol. This patrol would end at 4 a.m. when they were relieved by George McDonald and William H. Murphy who would patrol until sunrise. The barometer stood at 30.30 inches and the temperature was 22°. By sunrise the barometer was holding steady at 30.30 inches, but the temperature had fallen to 18°. The wind direction, weather and condition of the surf were the same as midnight. The surf remained strong throughout the day. The temperature had risen to 32° by noon and was the same at the sunset reading. By noon the wind had shifted to the southwest; the weather was fair. At sunset the wind was light from the southeast, the barometer remained high, and the weather had become cloudy. Surfmen Barber and Quinn were on the sunset to 8 p.m. patrol while Flynn and Wherity would patrol from 8 p.m. until midnight.

Fourth Cliff Life-Saving Station. Note the Fourth Cliff in Background. Photo courtesy of Cynthia Krusell.

Richard Wherity stood the day watch and had observed 11 schooners, 7 steamers and 1 sloop. Fred Stanley was on leave from 9:30 a.m. until 4:30 p.m..[4] Barber, who was in charge while Stanley was on leave, and the rest of the crew swept the house throughout and cleaned all the brass and iron work. According to the keeper's report the house was in good repair and thoroughly clean and the apparatus was in good condition.

Events happened in the next twenty-four hours that changed Humarock forever.

---

[4] Was Stanley aware of the approaching storm and taking his leave before things got bad- - we don't know.

CHAPTER 6

Point Allerton, Brant Rock and Gurnet Stations
STORM MINUS ONE DAY AND COUNTING

"But Captain James will always be regarded, by those who go down to the sea in ships, as the Patron Saint of Lifesavers." Dr. William M. Bergan

---

HULL

Joshua James was born in 1826 in Hull, Massachusetts. The sea had been the center of his life from the time he was 10 when his mother was lost in a shipwreck. Five years later he joined the Humane Society of Massachusetts. He had been a volunteer with the Humane Society for nearly a half century when he decided he wanted to enter the United States Life-Saving Service. The problem was he was too old by 17 years! Federal officials found it easy to look the other way and appoint him keeper of the Hull station because of his unparalleled record of saving lives -- a record that will never be shattered -- some 540 people!

" Practiced with the Beach Apparatus, Saturdays cleaning done and brass cleaned," wrote Joshua James on November 26, but

Hull Life-Saving Station looking toward Boston Light. Photo courtesy of Richard Cleverly.

James had no reason to expect anything other than an uneventful day. He noted at sunrise there was a fresh breeze form the west. There was only a slight chop on Boston Harbor. It was an unusually cold morning for that time of year with temperatures in the low 20s although the bright early morning sun promised a pleasant day.

James noted the barometer had changed little over the last 24 hours. At sunset it read 29.99 inches. The seas had been flat the whole day with a slight wind through noon from the west. The weather had been clear in the morning, but clouds had moved in by afternoon. At sunset the wind had shifted to the northeast.

Surfman Francis Mitchell had the day watch and observed 13 schooners, 18 steamers and 2 sloops pass by Point Allerton station. The other surfmen, Matthew Hoar, Fernando Bearse, George Pope, Martin Quinn, and James Murphy, had made their daily patrols. Although the log forms did not have a section for entering telephone calls received, all stations were connected by telephone and at some point during the morning James must have gotten word of the impending storm.

BRANT ROCK LIFE-SAVING STATION

Benjamin B. Manter was the keeper of the Brant Rock Station which was located in Marshfield near the old Union Chapel. Manter had a staffing problem that day. One surfmen was away from the station due to family illness and Manter obtained Arthur Manter for his substitute. Surfmen Baker was on the day watch and noticed heavy traffic passing by including 23 schooners and 3 steamers. The other members of the station held a routine resuscitation drill.

A comparison of the South Shore station logs shows an interesting pattern of higher wind speeds at the two most southerly stations. Manter recorded moderate winds from the west while

his counterparts to the north had observed lighter winds. The Brant Rock station apparently was just enough closer to the approaching storm for the winds to be somewhat stronger. However, as the day wore on the seas along that section of the coast had not become any rougher. The barometer at the station had been steady all day until late afternoon when it began to fall slightly. Shortly after sunset Manter knew his night might be busy. What an understatement!

GURNET LIFE-SAVING STATION

photo courtesy of Richard Boonisar

The Gurnet Station was located at the south end of Duxbury Beach at the entrance to Plymouth Harbor.

The keeper of this station was Augustus R. Rogers and of the 5 station keepers he wrote the most detailed account of the daily activities relating to personnel and patrols run. The surfmen and their position number under his command were:

#1 G.L. Nixon	#4 T. P. Stanley
#2 N.T. King	#5 A. Rohdin
#3 E.G. Tobin	#6 W. D. Kezer.

Rogers logged that since midnight on the 25th a strong sea had been running off the Gurnet. Winds that had been blowing from the west the night before had swung around to the northeast about 30 mph by sunset. Surfman Tobin kept the day watch and observed 28 schooners, 2 steamers, and 10 sloops pass by the station. Surfmen King and Kezer went to town in the dory to pick up the mail. They were gone about 4 hours.

When Rogers wrote the following, he didn't realize his door problem would be a minor

p. 29

inconvenience compared to what would follow the next day. "Boatroom doors would not stay locked, had to make them fast with rope, to keep them secure through the gale, which came in after sunset."

Augustus B. Rogers, Keeper.

Brig.

Topsail Schooner.

Fore-and-aft Rigged Schooner.

CHAPTER 7
Alert Disregarded

"The beach between the third and fourth cliff, is composed of sand and pebbles, and resists the attrition of the tides more than the cliffs: yet it is slowly wasting, and the river probably will eventually find its outlet between these cliffs."
                                        Samuel Deane, 1831

Surfman Richard Wherity knew that Saturday's routine at the Fourth Cliff Life-Saving station would have to wait, for signs indicated that a serious storm was heading his way. He worried about the hunters in their gunning shanties on the marshes along the North River. His first job today would be to warn them about the approaching storm.

An extensive marsh system lay just behind the Fourth Cliff in Humarock. Throughout the town's history these marsh areas were considered valuable, so much so, that the town of Scituate petitioned Plymouth Colony's government in early colonial times for more marshes because the land was poor for farming. The request was granted.

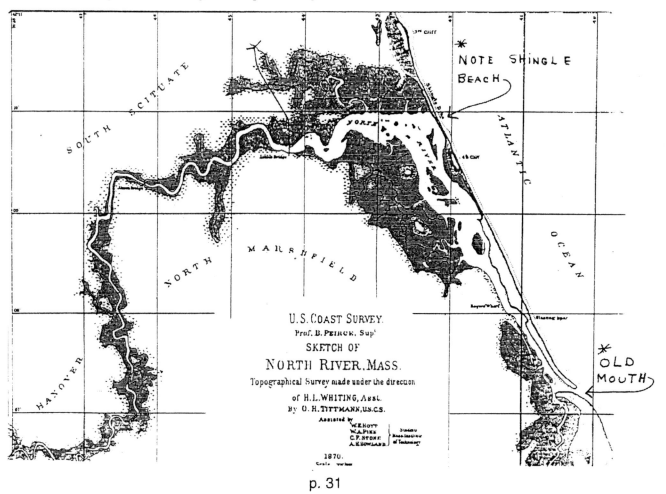

In the 1890's the marshes were prized by hunters and salt hay gatherers. Two specific hunting shanties of the many that were located there are of interest to our story. The first was owned by the Clapp family of Greenbush and the other by the Hendersons of Norwell. The Clapp's shanty was on the edge of the South River at the foot of Snake Hill in Marshfield while the Henderson shanty was just up river behind the Fourth Cliff.

The Thanksgiving holiday had just ended, and then, like now, it was a time for family. The Saturday after the holiday found three Clapp brothers, Everett, William H., and nineteen-year-old Richard, enjoying the hunt and weather. William was an avid hunter, and Everett had a flock of tame Canada geese that he used as live decoys. On November 26, they were nestled in their shanty awaiting the coot. The idea of a winter nor'easter was the farthest thing from their minds.

Upriver in their shanty five friends also enjoyed companionship and the hunting as well. They were Fred and Bert Henderson, Albert Tilden, George Ford, and a Webster boy. The Hendersons were probably regaling their friends with stories about their salt-haying business, their square-ended gundalow, girl friends, and other items of social interest to men in their twenties. All these boys were well-known and well-liked.

The Henderson brothers and Albert Tilden.

George Woodman was staying at his house on Trouant Island, which is just west of the Fourth Cliff. He recalled that the Henderson camp was just north of the island on a low rise. He could see the boys out hunting on the marsh that afternoon. He observed that they had shot some

geese, and since Woodman and his friends hadn't shot any he decided to go to their shanty and see if he could buy one for Sunday dinner. He went, but when he got there Woodman found that one boy had left and taken the geese with him. Woodman assumed that someone from Norwell had come down and persuaded

Photo courtesy of Cynthia Krusell.

one or two of the boys to leave. Actually it was Wherity of the Fourth Cliff Life-Saving station had warned them. He used the station's boat and visited the Hendersons' shanty and told them about the threatening weather forecast. George Webster left with him and returned to the Fourth Cliff Life-Saving station, the others decided to remain. This all happened prior to Woodman's arrival.

The Annual Report of the United States Life-Saving Service Fiscal Year Ending June 30, 1899, stated, "That stormy weather was threatening during the afternoon and early evening of November 26 is not within dispute. . . . But that the storm which followed far exceeded the apprehensions, both of the most timid and most intelligent, is equally clear."

In view of this report we can only imagine what it was like at the Henderson shanty, but we do know what happened at the Clapps. As the storm progressed and intensified, and when the water reached their armpits, the three Clapp brothers left their shanty in their small boat and made for land. But the raging storm waters were too turbulent. Their small boat was in imminent danger of sinking when a large, stray gundalow[5] swept by. The brothers leaped into it just as their boat sank. The Clapps were up to their waists in cold water, and without oars they were unable to steer their craft. Luckily the surging waters carried the boat toward Marshfield. Before the Clapp brothers arrived there, they heard cries for help and saw the Henderson brothers being swept away in their boat. Frustrated because they could not maneuver the gundalow to aid them, the Clapps

---

[5] It was a crude boat thirty to forty feet long, ten to twelve foot beam, that would hold three to eight tons of salt meadow hay. It was propelled by poles or sweep oars, and was floated with the tide. This was surely a word of the South Shore and North River country.

were forced to leave the Hendersons to their fate.

After striking land the Clapp brothers made for the Marshfield Hills Railroad Station. It was located on Macomber's land at Macomber's Island Road. Today this is Damon's Point Road. At the station Richard had to have his boots cut off and his feet rubbed. After being given brandy to warm them up, they started for home.

Travel was very dangerous. When they reached Little's Bridge, today the 3A bridge, it was covered with debris and the current moved so quickly that it was impossible to swim across there. They trudged through the snow to Union Street Bridge in Norwell and crossed there. By 3 p.m. they reached Greenbush, and were joyfully reunited with the rest of the family, for a few hours earlier the family had been told that the shanty had washed away and the brothers lost. Desperate to help, little Elijah T. Clapp Jr., the youngest of the Clapp brothers, had attempted to get to the Life-Saving station at Fourth Cliff, but he had been unable to do so. The reason being that the water had broken through the beach, so he could not pass. The storm was so intense that on his return trip home Elijah spent most of the time crawling on his hands and knees.

George Woodman recalling the storm's ferocity wrote, "Our house was the only one left and it washed off our piazza."

For the remainder of the afternoon and into the night the storm raged. Keeper Stanley would write that it was impossible to patrol from 8 p.m. until 4 a.m. He said, " During the gale this day the flag pole was blown [down] the out-building was moved off from its foundation and a lot of shingles torn off, and the platforms were washed away with the steps of the station; and a key post with one key." What Stanley described next in his log was almost beyond belief, for the beach that had joined Humarock to the rest of Scituate was gone!!!

A break had been blasted through the shingle beach and the course of the river dramatically altered. What he witnessed possibly had not been seen since the Great Hurricane of August 1635. Stanley was finally able to reach Scituate Harbor on Tuesday, he informed the citizens that their coastline had been changed forever. In his log for the November 27 he recorded, " The beach a little north of this Cliff is cut through so that it is impossible to get across except with a boat and then only occassionaly. Patroled the beach all day as far as it was possible to go as there was a large quantity of wreckage washing ashore all day. Fred Stanley, Keeper." The break through the beach north of the station

New inlet immediately after storm.

had made Humarock an island!

During the storm surfman Richard Wherity's duty also took him to Hatch's Gunning Shanty [three-quarters of a mile south of Fourth Cliff] where he saved David Sears. They struggled along the Hummocks until they reached Humarock Bridge. The bridge swayed back and

The bridge and the Hotel Humarock. Photo courtesy of Cynthia Krusell.

forth due to the gale and the surging water. Wherity managed to get Sears safely across the bridge to the Marshfield side. Wherity recrossed the bridge, which actually withstood the tempest, and braving fierce winds and wind-driven sand struggled back to the Life-Saving station. Keeper Stanley's report for November 28, 1898 summarized the aftermath, " Spent the day in clearing away the wreckage about the premises and looking for any bodies that might come ashore."

For two days the Clapp boys and others searched for the bodies of their friends. Woodman noted that on Monday morning, "about 11 o'clock we saw a boat coming down the river filled with men. They saw us and you can visualize their feelings when they saw that the Henderson house had been washed away, but apparently the four boys were safe on the island. It was a very different story when they came ashore. Two of the men were too weak to walk. Very distressing." Ann Rosini Clapp wrote, "Some men found the Ford body [November 29]. I expect the boys any

p. 35

moment and I hope they have found them all."

All the drowning victims bodies from the Henderson shanty were discovered. Albert Tilden's body was found on December 1 and the Hendersons were found December 2. At the joint funeral for the Henderson brothers and Albert Tilden a poem written by Miss Edna Clapp was read. In part it said:

In Memoriam

Each of us who died, now sends this, to comfort all his friends;

What ye lift upon the bier

Is not worth a single tear,

' Tis an empty sea shell, one

out of which the pearl is gone.

The shell is broken, it lies there;

The pearl, the all, the soul is here.

Farewell friends, but not farewell,

Where we are, ye too shall dwell.[6]

One final irony, the gundalow that saved the Clapps was owned by the Henderson brothers! It had broken loose during the storm!

---

[6] From "My Scituate" by Margaret Bonney.

CHAPTER 8
Anxiety and Heartache: The Columbia & Varuna

" I cannot believe he's dead," wife of Francis Nelson, steward on the pilot boat Columbia, November 28, 1898.

Immediately after the loss of the pilot boat Columbia and the steamer Portland there was much discussion and debate as to when and how they met their fates. The story of the Portland is discussed in Chapter 11. Since there were no survivors from either ship, it will never be known

The Columbia was considered by some to be lucky vessel with the number 2 displayed on her sail.

exactly what transpired on either of these vessels that awful night so many years ago.

In 1898 there were eight pilot boats that searched the waters off Boston for incoming vessels requiring a pilot to navigate them past the harbor's many hazards. Even today Boston pilots provide this necessary service. Piloting was a lucrative business in 1898 and boat owners took pride in their fast and expensive boats to conduct their enterprise. Competition was stiff among these boats and any trick that worked to place aboard a pilot was employed! One common shenanigan was to reverse running lights to confuse the competition. By doing so a competitor would believe a pilot was "manned out" and heading back to Boston when in fact she was sailing in the opposite direction! Imagine trying that stunt today! During daylight it was easy to identify each boat because a large number was displayed on the mainsail.

Some of these boats were especially noteworthy in appearance and structural integrity, pilot boats Columbia #2 and Varuna #6 being good examples. The Columbia was particularly pleasing

to the eye with her clipper type stern.[7] The Columbia was 89 tons, 85 feet long, and valued at $12,000. She was built at the Ambrose Martin Yard in East Boston in 1895. The Varuna was slightly older, built in 1892, but still considered very seaworthy.

The Varuna was on station a good distance off shore somewhere between Minot's Light and Provincetown under the command of William Fairfield on November 26 when the storm struck. How much Fairfield and his crew knew of the approaching storm is not known. What is known however, is that the captain had always had complete confidence in the integrity of his ship.

The Columbia had gone on station outside Boston Harbor a few days before the gale hit. At the beginning of her duty, four pilots were on board in addition to her crew of five. On Saturday, only pilot William Abbott, had yet to be placed on an incoming vessel.

The Columbia came upon the steamer Ohio which was nearing Massachusetts Bay from England.[8] With Abbott aboard the Ohio, the Columbia was now "manned out". When Abbott left the Columbia, Harry Peterson was in command. Abbott would be the last to see the Columbia crew alive.

Being far off shore, the Columbia may not have been fully aware of the approaching disaster, but certainly by midnight Saturday the Columbia's crew knew they were in trouble. The howling northeast winds demanded that sails be reefed, but soon the wind tore loose the reefing lines and the sails were quickly torn to shreds. When that happened Peterson lost all ability to maneuver the Columbia in the ever building seas.

Hour by hour the Columbia was driven closer to the Scituate shore. At some point during the storm the Columbia dropped both anchors hoping the ship could avoid the inevitable. That is a known fact because both chains were found extended after she beached at Cedar Point, but when did she actually smash ashore? Was it during the morning tide, or did she manage to stave off her tragic end until the evening tide? The same question has been repeatedly asked regarding the steamer Portland. The answer to the Columbia question is easier to determine.

Testimony by Richard Tobin who had passed by the spot where the Columbia crashed ashore just before high tide on the morning of November 27 gives part of the answer. He stated, "I went down the beach to the key post about three miles from the station. When I started from the station there was much wreckage on the beach, and the seas were coming over with such force that I was washed into the pond in back of the ridge [Musquashcut Pond]. It was blowing so hard that I was obliged to kneel down at times to get my breath. It was a hurricane from the northeast, and snowing so that I could not see any distance offshore. I kept on, and I had to take the fields back of the beach. Then I was able to make better progress, and at last reached the post, and then started to return. I warned a number of people in houses nearby that they had better seek safety elsewhere, as the seas were breaking up against the windows. I helped two families -- the women and children -- to a safe place in another house, and also assisted a fisherman to haul his boats away out of

---

[7] In 1773 an 83 foot ship named the Columbia was built on the North River. That Columbia became famous as the first American vessel to circumnavigate the globe. She also discovered the Columbia River in Oregon.

[8] The Ohio later grounded at Spectacle Island in Boston Harbor.

danger. When I was through with these things I started for the station and had to travel along the fields, it being impossible to keep to the beach. I got back to the station a little after half-past three in the afternoon." Tobin also testified that he had stood on the very porch of the cottage the Columbia struck.

Although there were no witnesses, it is almost guaranteed she came ashore during the Sunday morning tide. Three facts point to that scenario. The Sunday evening tide had a predicted height of only 8.9 feet, not sufficient water to drive the Columbia that high onto the beach. The winds by mid-evening had swung around to the north by northwest blowing somewhat offshore and a Mr. O'Hern, a fisherman, who was in a store in the Harbor, later testified that he heard a ship had come ashore at Sandhills, but that report never reached the North Scituate Life-Saving Station.

The afternoon patrol from that station was canceled since no vessel had been reported in need of assistance in the Scituate area, and the severe weather conditions made walking the beaches hazardous.

The midnight Sunday patrols did not begin until 1:00 a.m. due to high surf before that time. John Curran Jr. on the 4:00 a.m. to sunrise patrol came upon the Columbia at the neck of Cedar Point. The pilot boat was driven high on the beach, her foremast gone, the starboard side badly damaged, the anchor chains extended and anchors missing.[9] The body of one crewman lay in the hold. The surfman hurried back to the station and alerted George Brown, keeper. He immediately dispatched three surfmen for the wreck. A search of the area was conducted and four more bodies were found. The entire crew was lost, most likely drowning before the Columbia reached the beach.

Keeper Brown of the North Scituate Life Saving Station wrote in the November 28 log, "The watch started out at 1 a.m. after the sea went down so as not to come over the beach, the 4 a.m. to sunrise patrol came and reported that the pilot boat Columbia was ashore on top of the beach with both masts gone and no one there. Patrol took three of the crew and went down to her they told me that there was no one life but they found one body in the hold we pick one body up when we went down and saw one in the surf but could not get it so patrol left 2 of the crew down to watch for them and went back to the station and sent three down to relieve them they saw three in the surf but could not get them."

The worst fears of those that worked the Boston waterfront were now confirmed. Their hopes that the Columbia had somehow survived the storm were destroyed by the monstrous seas off Scituate.

A Boston Post reporter visited the home of Mrs. Frank Nelson at 15 Charter Street in Boston on the evening of the 28th. He found Nelson's wife and daughters extremely distraught by the news that Nelson had perished on the Columbia. The Nelsons had recently lost their son, Martin aged 17, and this latest news was more than she and the other family members could bear or accept. She told the reporter, " Never before in all these thirty years of seafaring life has he met

---

[9] Much of the hull damage probably occurred as the Columbia struck Long Ledge off Sandhills.

The Boston Daily Globe.

BOSTON, MONDAY EVENING, NOVEMBER 28, 1898 TWELVE PAGES. PRICE TWO CENTS.

GLOBE LATEST---7.30 P M.

COLUMBIA WRECKED

Boston Pilot Boat Piled Up on the Beach at Scituate.

CREW OF FIVE MEN DROWNED

with a mishap"- - "He had followed the sea since a boy and most of that time as a steward. He is 45 years of age now and when he was ten he started out and first became cabin boy. Most of that time he has been in coastwise vessels and for a few years on board a pilot boat. Everybody could not help liking him, as he was good. I cannot believe he's dead and with Martin only buried it is terrible."[10]

The five lost were popular and respected mariners. All of the crew were of Scandinavian descent and were a closely knit group. The known names of the men drowned are: Peter Peterson age 42, first boatkeeper; Edward Patterson age 22, second boatkeeper; Andrew Ellingsen age 37, third boatkeeper who resided at North Bennet Street, Boston; the fourth boatkeeper was unknown according to papers of that time; Frank Nelson, steward, Charter Street, Boston.[11]

While the fate of the Columbia was now known, friends of the Varuna's crew still held out some small hope theVaruna had survived, but as the hours passed without any word of her, the fact that a board bearing her name had been found on Cape Cod, and the rapidly expanding list of ships lost, caused them to accept the inevitable.

On Tuesday they had the answer, but first a brief description of events. When the storm began its increased fury, Captain William Fairfield instructed that he be lashed near the wheel where he remained for twenty-four hours. During that time her rigging was badly damaged and her lee rail swept away. With his ribs broken, and knowing Fairfield could not take further punishment from the onslaught of the seas, the crew cut him loose and dragged him below. Typical of an old salt he yelled, "Keep her headed up, make a straight wake: She is made of oak and copper and can stand it."

---

[10] Francis Nelson by some accounts had been out of work and this was his first trip in some time. He was a very popular man on the Boston waterfront, known for his commitment to the job as a good cook.
[11] In an ironic twist of history Edward McNabb is the present owner of the property where the Columbia grounded. He resides on Charter Street, Boston!

On Tuesday, November 29 the Philadelphia, sailing for Boston came upon the Varuna. She was of course badly damaged, but afloat. The Philadelphia took the Varuna in tow and late in the day entered Boston Harbor. When they arrived, they were met by cheers and whistles all along the inner harbor -- One of the few happy endings of this terrible carnage.

The house to right of bowsprit was righted and repaired.

Note Columbia's extended anchor chains.

p. 41

CHAPTER 9

Bravery at Black Rock

" The sea at times would strike the wall, break over, and bury men, beach apparatus and all making it very

disagreeable and dangerous. . . ." Joshua James

The full force of the cyclonic storm would be felt on the 27th of November. It would strain Joshua James and his crew to their limit, but at the same time it would become their finest hour.

During the two-day storm James and his men rescued men from wrecked vessels, took in and cared for not only the rescued men, but a family whose house was in danger during the gale, and kept up their patrols. For 48 hours James and his crew were kept busy.

HENRY R. TILTON

The harrowing story was launched with Joshua James's report, "About 3 o'clock this morning during the severe N.E. snow storm and gale, through the rift in the snow, a vessel was seen at anchor nearly abreast of the station 1/4 mile away. At four o'clock she had dragged ashore near Toddy Rocks 1/3 mile N.W. of the Station about 500 yds. off shore. There was a terrific gale and it was impossible to launch the boat." The vessel was the Henry R. Tilton from Norfolk, Virginia. She was carrying lumber bound for Boston. Captain Cobb and 6 men made up the crew. "About 6:30 a.m. she had worked in close enough to throw a line across her. The first shot fired fell across her jib stay. The crew succeeded in getting hold of it." Because there was so much wreckage, rocks, seaweed and kelp, the line could not be drawn any more than halfway to the ship. Two additional shots were attempted, the last one being successful. The rope was hauled in

p. 42

by the crew, and the breeches buoy operation began. One man was brought ashore.

The report continued, " It was fully three hours before we got them ashore, notwithstanding, we were assisted by the Mass. Humane Society volunteer crew, and many others." James in his report explained the danger of this part of the rescue, "In the vicinity where this occured there is a heavy granite sea wall. The men handling the whip line and hawser were obliged to stand on the edge of this wall to keep the line clear of rocks, seaweed and wreckage. The sea at times would strike the wall, break over, and bury men, beach apparatus and all making it very disagreeable and dangerous also difficult to see when the men got into the breeches buoy."

The rescued crew stayed four days at the lifesaving station. They consumed 54 meals during their stay which was paid for by the owners of the vessel.

top and bottom photos courtesy of Richard Cleverly.

COAL BARGES NO. 1 & 4

While James and his crew were rescuing the crew of the Henry Tilton, James received word that a coal barge was dragging ashore about 3/4 of a mile further north near Toddy Rocks.

" As it would require some time to get other beach apparatus from the station, on account of the very heavy sea, wreckage, telegraph poles, wires, etc. that was working about and around

the Station, the keeper of the Mass. Humane Society sent for horses to take his beach apparatus there, the two crews going together, it being impossible for one to do anything alone."

The combined crews fired two shots from the Hunt gun, but were unsuccessful. The situation was becoming desperate because the barge was breaking up. There was only one way to save them. James had some of his men tie ropes around themselves while the remaining members of the crew held on to the ends of the ropes. Then the so-tied surfmen waded into the frenzied surf.

James continued, " The house [on the coal barge] these men were on broke away from the deck of the barge, and came into the breakers, the men being thrown in a heap, into the surf, near enough for our men to seize them and hold them from going back in the undertow, and as the next sea came they all came up safely together. The crew was in a helpless condition, and had to be taken bodily and carried to a cottage near by."

The rescuers broke into the cottage and cared for the crew there. The vessel was coal barge number 1 bound for Boston from Baltimore with a cargo of coal valued at $4,000. Captain Joshua Thomas, Charles Machale, Jacob Hines, Alfred Nickerson, and Paul Steffanowski comprised her crew. They had 25 meals while at the Point Allerton Station.

Another coal barge, barge number 4, wasn't as lucky. She had come ashore during the night, but the wreckage washed up on the beach at 5 a.m.. Two men rescued themselves and took shelter at the home of Mr. Cleverly, which was near Toddy Rocks. Later in the afternoon they were taken to the Station and were cared for there. The other three members of the crew perished. No one knew the barge had foundered until the wreckage washed up on the shore.

ABEL E. BABCOCK

A schooner from Baltimore, the Abel E. Babcock, also carrying coal to Boston, was lost with all hands. Joshua James reported, " This vessel probably struck on the outer ledge of Toddy Rocks,

Photo courtesy of Richard Cleverly.

and went to pieces. Did not know about it until the wreckage came ashore at daylight. None of the

p. 44

bodies belonging to this vessel have been picked up at this date." The report was written on December 14, 1898.

CALVIN F. BAKER

The second day of the tempest James and his men rescued three men from a schooner, then saved three men from Black Rock. The schooner was the Calvin F. Baker. She was carrying coal to Boston from Baltimore. There were eight in the crew including Captain J. Megathlin. Five would be saved, but tragically three lost their lives.[12] "This vessel was seen late in the afternoon of Nov. 27 [NEAR

Note Calvin Baker in the distance. Photo courtesy of Richard Cleverly.

BOSTON LIGHT] but it was impossible for any boat to go there in the hurricane and heavy sea. At day break Nov. 28 looked with the glass to see if the Light Keeper had signals, having arranged previously with him to make signals in case of disaster, & saw the signal and at once launched the Mass. Humane Society's life boat, taking four volunteers.[13] Signaled to a tug boat for a tow. The tug boat "Ariel" took us near the island as he dared go, we had to pass several breakers, over a bar, but succeeded and got along side where it as comparatively smooth. Took off five men, (and one dead body, the mate and second mate were drowned). Put them in the tug boat where they were furnished with hot drinks. The tug then towed us back. Took the crew to the station, provided them with dry clothing food, and sent the body to the morgue. She got ashore about 3 o'clock Sunday morning. There was but a small portion of the deck forward where the crew could stand, the remainder being washed away, at high water were obliged . . . into the rigging. This crew were in pitiable condition for 30 hours. Two of the men's feet were badly swollen being jammed and frost bitten. Had medical treatment," Joshua James.

Two additional facts need mention here. First, the keeper of the Mass Humane Station was Osceola James, who was Joshua's son. Second, Joshua James was seventy-two years of age when he performed these incredible feats of courage and endurance.

---

[12] They were the steward Willis H. Studley, mate Burgess Howland, and the second mate whose name was unknown.

[13] This was because the seas were so dangerous.

p. 45

Now on to Cohasset and the rescue at Black Rock.

BLACK ROCK

A heroic but failed attempt by the Humane Society's crew. Photo courtesy of John Salvador.

As soon as James and his crew returned from the Calvin Baker at 10:30 a.m. Monday, they were informed five men were stranded on Black Rock which is off the Hull-Cohasset border. They immediately departed for the scene, some six miles from their station.

When they arrived, they found the crew of the Cohasset Humane Society had made a valiant but unsuccessful attempt to reach the rock; they had been thrown from the boat by high rollers still smashing ashore. Fortunately none of these rescuers drowned. The Humane crew was comprised of: William Brennock, Antoine Salvador, Albert Morris, John E. Frates, Frank Salvador, George E. Antoine, Joseph J. Grassie, James A. Brennock, Frank Martin Jr., and Manuel Salvador. These men were well known and respected in Cohasset. Each was subsequently paid $10 by the Humane Society of the Commonwealth of Massachusetts for their effort.

James assessed the situation and determined that to avoid the same fate as the first attempt, it would be necessary to wait another hour and hope the seas abated. Finally the surf seemed to slacken and the boat was launched, but to make a landing, remove the men, and pull away from the rock was a dangerous maneuver.

James later wrote, " We succeeded in launching, rowing one mile to the rock.[14] As it was very difficult to land, with the heavy sea breaking around the rock, we had to wait an hour or more, watching for a favorable opportunity to make a landing. When the chance presented itself

[14] James's landing was done from Gun Rock Cove.

Hull Life-Saving crew rescue
of Nichols crew at Black Rock.

The Hull Life-Saving Station
on the way to Black Rock.
Photo courtesy of David
Wadsworth.

made a strong pull landing safely on the rock. Got the men three in number on board and again waited a favorable chance to launch which we did just before sundown."

The rescued had broken in to a small cottage on Black Rock used for hunting and had built a fire to keep warm. When James got the men ashore, he learned they were from the Lucy A. Nichols, one of two barges carrying coal in tow by the tug Underwriter.[15] They had been cut loose off Minot's Light during the storm. The sister barge, Virginia, was not as lucky and was lost.

THE JUNIATA, COHASSET
There was only one large vessel grounded at Cohasset, the Juniata. She was a fishing schooner less than a year old with a value of $10,000. The crew of seventeen under the command of Captain R.M. Corey had worked hard

[15] The three members of the crew were lucky. When the barge grounded near the rock, they quickly scrambled to it. The captain and mate tried the same, but lost their grip and drowned.

before the storm, having caught 14,000 pounds of fish.

The night of the storm the Juniata was northeast of Cohasset in about 120' of water. At midnight Corey ordered both anchors dropped and for the next 45 minutes the Juniata was riding well. However, just before 1 a.m. huge waves crashed over her and the anchor cables parted. Corey's next tactic was to hoist a riding sail to give him steerage with the hope he could somehow make Cohasset Harbor. It wasn't long before the sail was quickly torn apart by the fierce winds. That put the Juniata at the sea's mercy. Captain Corey stayed at the wheel, and the crew clambered into the rigging, lashing themselves there. After two hours Corey realized he too must join them.

At 4:00 a.m. the Juniata struck rocks and the terrified crew awaited their end, but miraculously she was lifted over them by the next wave. The schooner was then driven ever closer to shore over the next few minutes until she landed against a breakwater on Beach Island. The crew was able to scramble from the rigging to the safety of the shore.[16] The crew then entered Mr. Nicholas Sheldon's cottage nearby, and made a fire and warmed themselves for the first time in many hours.

The facts that she drew only ten feet of water and that she had landed on the rocks, which are bare at low tide, convinced many Cohasset mariners that the tide did not ebb much that night. With seas coming higher and higher the tide rose, the Juniata was lifted clean over the breakwater and deposited near Mr. Sheldon's piazza.

The escape of this vessel is remarkable, for had she struck 100 feet to either side, she would have been dashed to pieces on the savage rocks. The breakwater suffered damage to its wooden planking where the Juniata had struck it.

---

[16] At high tide the Juniata moved once more, when she was lifted over the breakwater and driven even further up the beach.

Later after this ordeal, the crew of the Juniata were taken to the Cohasset firehouse where they were given dry clothes and food.

Fire House at Elm and South Main Sts., looking southeast, Cohasset. Now used as a teen center.

CHAPTER 10

Lost! Daniel I. Tenney, Mertis Perry & the Edgar Foster

"The arm of the Lord hath made the depths of the sea a way for the ransomed to pass over." Isaiah 51:10

FURY OF GALE
Massachusetts Bay One Vast Mass of Wreckage

The lifesaving crew report the wreck of a large barge, ashore at Humarock beach. It is thought to be the Daniel I. Tenney of Boston. No trace of the crew has been found yet.

(Quincy Daily Ledger- Tuesday, November 29, 1898)

DANIEL I. TENNEY

Wrecks were strewn everywhere along the coastline of Massachusetts. The toll taken in human lives lost was horrendous. The story of the Daniel Tenney is just one of the hundreds of tragic tales that the gale created.

The Daniel I. Tenney was a barge that was laden with coal. Its journey began in Newport News, Virginia. Her destination was Boston. The Captain of the Tenney was J.F. Cox, and he was accompanied by his wife and four crew members. It was owned by the Boston Towboat Company. A sister barge Delaware was also being towed, and she had a crew of six.

The ocean tug Mars picked up the two barges early on November 26 off Handkerchief lightship, Nantucket Shoals and headed north. Captain Miles of the Mars recorded this in the log:

At 3 p.m. they passed Chatham on Cape Cod, at 7 p.m. they cleared the Cape and were headed to Boston.

According to the log at 8:40 p.m. the Mars struck snow squalls. The wind was from the east southeast. By 11 p.m. the gale force wind and heavy seas concerned the Captain and his mate. Captain Miles and Mate Magee later said that in all their 30 years at sea they have never passed through such a storm.

At 12:15 a.m. November 27 the wind was blowing a hurricane and the tugs slowed down to take soundings. The snow was so thick and visibility so poor they could not see one foot in front them. Captain Miles believed they were off Minot's Light in 18 fathoms of water.

At 12:40 a.m. the captain made several unsuccessful attempts to bring the tow to the wind in order to anchor.

By 1 a.m. Captain Miles reported that the wind blew with such hurricane force that it was impossible for him to hold on to the tow. He signaled the barges to anchor. He thought that they

could ride out the storm because they both had good tackle, so he cut them loose.

The wind was blowing at 75 miles per hour and the seas were extremely heavy. The high seas broke over the tug and smashed the pilot house which flooded the cabin and filled the lower portion of the tug. She was now in real danger as water threatened to engulf the tug, but the pumps held their own and kept ahead of the water.

At 6:20 a.m. after striking bottom several times the captain believed they were on the northerly end of the Peaked Hill Bars. He thought they were lost, but a maneuver hard to port got them off.

After much hard work and many starts the Mars found itself in a lull off the leeward side of Billingsgate Island [on the inside of Cape Cod near Wellfleet]. It was a mystery as to how that got there because of the deadly shoals which surrounded this island.

For the rest of the night and all day Monday the tug remained there. The crew removed wreckage form the deck and water from the hold.

On Tuesday with a decrease in the wind and sea the tug got under way and hunted for the two barges, but found no sign.

The crew of the Fourth Cliff Life-Saving Station unsuccessfully searched the wreckage along Humarock for any bodies.[17]

WRECKS OFF SCITUATE

AT HUMAROCK THE BARGE DANIEL TENNEY, WHICH WAS ONCE KNOWN AS A STANCH SHIP, IS A HOPELESS WRECK, AND NO TRACE OF HER CREW HAVE YET BEEN FOUND.

(Boston Advertiser- November 30, 1898)

THE LOSS OF THE MERTIS PERRY-BRANT ROCK

During the morning of the storm the fishing schooner Mertis H. Perry came ashore two miles north of the Brant Rock Station and five of the fourteen men crew lost their lives-- two from exposure and three from drowning.

The Perry had left Boston the previous Monday afternoon for a week of fishing southeast of Highland Light, Cape Cod. Her trip had been uneventful except that on the 24th and 25th she sailed into Provincetown Harbor because of high northwest winds.

---

[17] Bruce Berman in the Encyclopedia of American shipwrecks lists the wreckage of the Tenney off Sandy Neck , Barnstable on Cape Cod. The Mars had a long and interesting career. She sank 9/13/42 off Plymouth under mysterious circumstances.

Photo courtesy of Cynthia Krusell.

On the evening of the 26th the Perry headed for Boston with a catch of 15,000 pounds of fish -- in today's economy equivalent to a conservative $15,000.

At 9:30 p.m. the Perry was engulfed in snow and wind. Captain Joshua Pike reefed the sails and set a course northwest by north, which he hoped would keep him on a general heading for Boston.

At 11:00 p.m. Pike was worried the Perry was not keeping that course and wore the ship in hopes of edging her more offshore, but during that manuever the main gaff broke and the jib split.[18] With the jib now useless, the Perry was not able to make any headway, so the sails were lowered and the port and starboard anchors let go. The increasing fury of the gale caused the anchors to drag and the ship drifted across ever shallower waters. Pike was desperate for some solution and next ordered the masts cut away. The foremast went first, but hung up on the jib stay. The mainmast fell clear.

About 2 a.m. Sunday the cable secured to the port anchor broke and the crew used the remaining length to increase the scope of the starboard anchor, but the dragging continued.

At 7:00 a.m. the starboard anchor finally grabbed, but almost immediately parted. Pike had no choice but to head her toward the beach and hope for the best. The crew clung to the stubs of the masts as the Perry dashed through breaking surf and ever closer to the beach.

At 8 a.m. William Bagnall, "gave up and died." Then the captain, "demented from his awful experience" grabbed the smashed dory and jumped overboard and was not seen again. The rush of the breakers forced the ship so far up on the beach ten of the crew were able to scramble from the jib boom to safety. However, one fell off and another died from exhaustion. Charles Forbes who made it to shore, "was so prostrated that the survivors were obliged to leave him behind" as they sought help.

---

[18] In sailing circles today this is known as an intentional Jibe- a dangerous manuever under the best of conditions.

The Annual Report of the United States Life-Saving Service for June 30, 1899 stated, "From the foregoing account it will be seen that nine men survived and five men perished. It was a sad catastrophe, which could not, under the circumstances, have been averted or made less fatal in its consequences by the efforts on the part of the Life-Saving crew of the Brant Rock Station. The conditions of the weather were such that it was utterly impossible for the life-savers to discover the vessel when she came ashore, much less to reach her in time to save life. . . ."

THE RESCUE OF ADMIRAL DEWEY FROM THE SCHOONER EDGAR FOSTER

Photo courtesy of Richard Boonisar.

The fishing schooner Edgar Foster of Bucksport, Me., loaded with herring, anchored off Portsmouth, N.H. on Saturday, but the howling northeast winds parted her from her mooring. There was nothing the crew could do as the Foster was driven southeast across Massachusetts Bay.

At 11:00 a.m. Sunday the Foster struck the shore broadside at Brant Rock and two of her crew were able to scramble ashore. A line was then thrown aboard and the others were rescued -- except for Admiral Dewey. The captain then returned to the ship to rescue the admiral. The admiral was found cowering under a bunk. Although he enjoyed many aspects of life at sea, being wet was not one of them. He was finally coaxed off and saved. Admiral Dewey was the ship's cat!!!!

WRECK OF THE EDGAR B. FOSTER AT BRANT ROCK.

GURNET

The Gurnet station was one of the most remote along the South Shore and a popular spot for hunters. This desolation also created dangers for vessels foundering there, for if shipwrecked crews were not discovered quickly they often perished.

Problems for keeper Augustus Rogers escalated after the boathouse door incident at the onset of the storm. Stations to the north at least had a respite the Tuesday after the storm; Rogers and his crew were out straight until the next Saturday. Rogers wrote:

November 27

"Between 8 & 12 a.m. Kezer patroled the beach 3 miles, could not get any further on account of the sea breaking over the beach, went to houses where there were some gunners, helped them to get their things away, the water then being 3 ft. deep on their floor."

"Put up at station 9 gunners who were driven out of their houses by the tide, supplied them with dry clothing. . . ."

"As soon as tide left so that we could go the west patrol, sent a man that way, met the Capt. of the Venus, who said hs sloop was ashore in Saquish Cove, (all hands safe) he also stated that there were eleven sails anchored off Saquish & Clark's Island (inside) last night, & only two now in sight, one being his, and the other the Charles W. Parker which was riding with both masts gone. I asked him if there was anything we could do for him, he said **"no living man could do anything on the water a day like this."**

"The surfman from the westward returned -- stated that he could not see anything on account of the snow, but said that the gunners there told him the sch. seemed to be riding all right the last

time they saw her. In the mean time an unknown sch. was sighted at anchor about 1/2 mile ENE from Gurnet Head, and being in a very dangerous place, all hands kept watch for her until night set in, then placed two men on watch, but she did not use any light, so that was the last we saw of her, at daylight was no where in sight."[19]

November 28

"Sent Stanley to Duxbury with mail, on his way back saw a body floating in the surf, got hold of it but could not secure it on account of such an undertow, returned to the station and reported, all hands then went up the beach, patroled the beach all night but failed to see any thing more of it."

"Gunners left for home today."

"High tide washed both boats away that we had picked up keeping for the owners."

The next day Rogers examined the old station, which had been built in 1873, for storm damage. He found it in worse shape then it had first looked. He noted that just about everything on the lower floor was gone except the boats. The boats looked to be all right. He also noticed that the upper floor had settled about three feet. He took the self bailer out and moved it to the new station, and he also moved the Monmoy boat outside.

Rogers also logged that the crew of the schooner Venus gave up the idea of staying on board. They asked him if he could put them up at the station. He agreed and fed and gave them beds.

BODY ON THE BEACH

Rogers recorded, " E. Tobin . . . did not meet the Brant Rock surfman on account of the beach being washed so bad went to Brant Rock Station, was so tired out, did not return until 6 a.m. this morning. On his return saw the body of a man on the beach. . . .but could not handle it alone, on account of its being almost buried in sand and seaweed, returned immediately to station. King and myself took station team and went to where the body lay. . . .found the head badly bruised, should say it had been dead surely 24 hours. We then rolled the body in one of station blankets. . . went to Town and delivered body to coroner E. Hill, Plymouth. He had black hair, none on top of head, blue eyes, 5 ft. 8 1/2 inches tall. One joint of the finger next to little finger gone on right hand."

On Wednesday a northeaster of impressive strength struck. Rogers cancelled the routine practice drills so the beaches could again be patrolled. The normal seclusion of the Gurnet was now even greater for the patrols from the station met no one from the Brant Rock Station. Rogers also noted the whistling buoy off Gurnet and the buoy off High Pine Ledge had been moved off location.[20]

Thursday and Friday were spent salvaging items of value from the old boathouse and repairing equipment. The crew at this time had to be near the point of exhaustion.

[19] What vessel this was is not known. This was one of scores of vessels that disappeared with their crews.
[20] It is not uncommon for navigation aids to drift off station. The bell buoy at the entrance to Scituate Harbor was moved in two recent storms: Blizzard of 1978 & 1991 No Name storm.

Saturday, December 3 was quiet and the difficult week was behind the men. The entire crew went to Plymouth to mail letters and pick up much needed food. The awful week had finally ended. One last entry though was a reminder that the effects of the storm still lingered, "Chief of Police of Plymouth, told me today that the body we picked up had not been identified. Augustus B. Rogers, Keeper."

WRECK AND DEATH.

Dire Destruction at Brant Rock and Green Harbor.

Two Vessels Lost, Five Men Perish and Many Cottages in Ruins.

Shipwreck on the sea, death in the waters and ruin on the land is the record of the storm at Brant Rock and Green Harbor. Two staunch schooners were lost, five hardy sailors gave up their crew at the command of the elements, and scores of houses were literally torn to fragments by the hurricane which prevailed.

No such storm ever before visited that section, and no such havoc was ever wrought, in the locality where many Bostonians spend the sunny summer months. After an all night struggle with the wind and the waves the two vessels were dashed upon the coast, and nothing but nerve and indomitable courage saved the crew of the schooner. The storm began, as elsewhere, mildly, but in a few hours had reached hurricane proportions, and at high tide Sunday forenoon there was no hope for the salvation of anything which floated in the vicinity.

The story of the storm's havoc at the points mentioned was brought to Boston last night by Mr. Asa C. Jewitt of Newton Centre, who, after an all day struggle with adverse conditions, reached the city.

Mr. Jewitt is the owner of cottages at Green Harbor and its vicinity, and, as was his frequent custom, went down to the shore Saturday night to look after his property. Yesterday morning he procured the only sleigh there was at Green Harbor and was driven to Green Harbor depot and then to Marshfield in a vain effort to find a train. He learned that half a mile of the New York, New Haven & Hartford railroad was washed out at Greenbush, and that there was another large washout near Duxbury. His first efforts failing, Mr. Jewitt obtained a driver and four horses at Marshfield and, after a 12-mile journey through the drifts, reached Hanover, where he took a train which landed him in Boston last evening.

He brought a message to Francis J. O'Hara & Co., who control the fishing schooner Myrtle H. Perry, from the mate of that vessel, announcing her wreck and the loss of the captain and four of the crew.

Saturday the Perry was fishing off Boston light, and anchored for noting the approach of the storm. Early in the night, however, the vessel dragged from her anchorage and until daylight was the plaything of the gale. About 7 o'clock Sunday morning the shore was sighted through the blinding snow, and a few minutes later the vessel drove head on to the beach at Rexham Terrace, above the Brant Rock life saving station.

Capt. Joshua Pike jumped overboard and made a heroic attempt to reach the shore with the hope of obtaining succor for his helpless crew. The wind and the waves were too strong for him, however, and he was swept away and drowned.

Then one of the crew undertook the almost hopeless task. He reached the land, but at the cost of his life, for he soon died from exhaustion. Three other men were also finishing their last cruise, for they were swept from the vessel and drowned.

The nine remaining members of the crew, headed by the mate, eventually got ashore, after the tide had gone down, in an exhausted condition. One

measure of control over the vessel failed, and, after a race horse drive along down the North Shore, she was buried on the rocks Sunday forenoon. First she struck the Brant Rock shoals, and 20 or 40 feet of her bottom was torn off, leaving a gaping hole in her side, into which the sea rushed with a roar. Over the shoals she slid, and in

Photo courtesy of Richard Boonisar.

p. 56

CHAPTER 11

Rendezvous with Destruction: The Loss of The Portland

"My soul waitheth for the Lord more than they that watch for morning." Psalm 130:6

It was 7 p.m. on that chill, gray Saturday when a steamship's whistle shattered the night around Atlantic Avenue Boston. The steamship Portland pulled slowly away from the famed India Wharf. She was making her daily eight hour run to Portland, and this being the Saturday after Thanksgiving many more passengers than usual had booked passage. But Portland was not to be her final destination; Eternity awaited her crew and passengers.

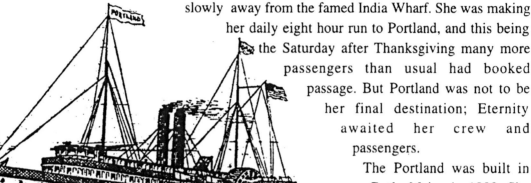

STEAMER PORTLAND.

The Portland was built in Bath, Maine in 1889. She was a beautiful ship and was considered one of the finest of her types. She was equipped with all the latest furnishings, including electric lighting. The following description appeared in the July 1, 1889 edition of the Bath Daily Times, "The main cabin will have the domed skylight while two octagon skylights will light the saloon forward. Here there will be a gallery and two tiers of staterooms. Along the side there will be Corinthian pilasters with Corinthian capitals. There will be 56 rooms on the hurricane deck and 168 below. Altogether there will be 514 berths. The finish in the staterooms is cherry. The deck is of 3 inch white pine. The main stairway, leading up from the main deck, will be of mahogany."

The Portland was a paddle-wheel steamer 280.9 feet long, 42.1 feet wide, but she was 26 feet wider across the paddle-wheel guards. Her draught was 10 feet 8 inches. She was powered by a walking beam engine of 1400 h.p. which allowed her a top speed of 15 miles per hour. Because of her shallow draft, the Portland was better suited for river rather than for ocean travel. This defect would become fatally apparent.

The central figure in this drama was Hollis Blanchard, Captain of the Portland. What do we know about him, what kind of person was he, and why did he sail knowing a storm was coming? He lived in Westbrook, Maine. He was married and had three children, two sons and a daughter. One of his sons lived in Boston. His daughter was about 19 years old. Blanchard had followed the

sea his whole life, and for ten years had worked for the Portland Steamship line, first as a pilot for the Portland and upon the recent death of Captain Snowman he was promoted to Captain. Obviously the company had confidence in his ability and judgment to promote him. He had the reputation of being reliable and had experience in handling side-wheelers. This experience with side-wheelers also made him aware of their unseaworthiness in rough ocean weather.

Excellent model of the Portland

Captain Blanchard became well-known to the men at the U.S. Weather Bureau in Boston since he often solicited their advice before sailing, and had become very friendly with the whole staff. They explained the weather map to him, and through discussions with the staff he learned about the wind direction and strength. If the wind was too strong from abeam, he wouldn't sail. Because he checked the daily weather maps, drew conclusions from discussions with the men of the Weather Bureau, and knew the Portland's weaknesses, he had earned a reputation for being cautious. So why did he sail when so many other vessels were seeking refuge? Was he ordered to because of increased competition from the railroads? Did he disobey company orders and sail anyway? Or did he truly believe he could outrun the storm?

The following three questions in addition to the ones raised already have raged ever since the sinking of the Portland. Where did Captain Blanchard head the Portland after he realized his plight? Where did she sink? Finally, when did she sink?

Saturday November 26

Some passengers must have had some trepidations regarding the weather, but they felt secure in Captain Blanchard's knowledge and experience. We know that Blanchard was aware of the

storm because in the afternoon he had a phone conversation with Captain Dennison, the captain of the Baystate--the Portland's sister ship. Captain Dennison had decided to stay in Portland, but Blanchard explained that he had decided to sail. At 5:30 p.m. John Liscomb, General Manager of the Portland Steamship Company, telephoned Boston from Portland and asked to speak to Captain Blanchard, but he could not be found. Liscomb told C.F. Williams, their Boston agent, that he wanted him to tell Captain Blanchard to hold the Portland until 9 p.m., and if the weather was threatening, to cancel the voyage. Liscomb requested Williams to advise Captain Blanchard to call Captain Dennison at 6 o'clock that afternoon. As requested, Williams with Blanchard standing beside him called Dennison at about 6 o'clock. Dennison gave him the Portland weather. Captain Blanchard told Williams to convey to Dennison his intention to sail on schedule in view of the weather indications which then existed. Captain Dennison replied that he had decided to stay in port until the 9 o'clock weather report. Just at that moment a telegram from a weather reporter in New York was handed to Williams who read it and handed it to Captain Blanchard. The telegram read, "Snowing. Wind North West." Blanchard left the office to go on board the steamer, but before leaving he said, " We are going to have the wind from the north west." At 7 p.m. the Portland sailed.[21]

After its 7 p.m. sailing the Portland was sighted by many people. At 7:20 p.m. the Portland was seen by the keeper of the Deer Island Light, Wesley Pinagree. As she turned to the open sea, she traded whistle signals with the Kennebec, which had sailed earlier but was returning to the

[21] We believe this telegram is what motivated Blanchard to sail. The wind direction convinced him that the storm was moving out to sea.

shelter of Boston because of the threatening weather. The Captain of the Sylph No. 8 saw both vessels while he was 8 miles from the Boston Lightship. The steamer Mt. Desert passed the Portland near Graves Ledges as it was entering Boston Harbor. Captain Roix of the Mt. Desert looked back expecting the Portland to turn around, but it continued on its way. A gentle, light snow had begun by 7:37 p.m., but by 8 p.m. the snow was swirling in the increasing wind.

An interesting story was related to Edward R. Snow by Captain Charles T. Martell of Medford, skipper of the tugboat Channing, fifty years later. He contends that, " I was steering the tugboat Channing in a southeasterly direction, and the weather began to spit snow about 8 o'clock. We were off Nahant. The weather was not bad at the time, but I knew a serious storm was coming.

"There were ten or twelve young men gathered on the topside of the Portland just forward and aft of the paddle wheel box. When one of the young bloods on the Portland shouted across to me to get my old scow out of the way, I shouted back at him, 'You'd better stop that hollering, because I don't think you'll be this smart tomorrow morning.'

"By this time I was less than 20 feet from the Portland, and could easily make out the features of the young men sailing to their death. I gave three blasts of the Channing's whistle, and Captain Blanchard, whom I could easily recognize in the wheel house, answered back."

Two hours later the Portland was on schedule off Bass Rocks about 4 miles southwest of Thatcher's Island. She was seen here by Master William Thomas of the schooner Maud S., who was making for Gloucester Harbor in the growing storm. About the same time or shortly thereafter Captain Lynes B. Hathaway, master workman of the Lighthouse Department, was in the smoking room of the Thatcher Island Lighthouse when he saw the Portland's lights as the steamer passed within 500 feet of the shore between Thatcher's and Londoner Ledge.

During the next two hours the storm would intensify quickly. By 11 p.m. the Portland was sighted 12 miles southeast of Thatcher's Island by the schooner Grayling, which was skippered by Reuben Cameron. The visibility was so poor that when Cameron realized the Portland was bearing down on his vessel, he lit a flare to apprise it of his presence. The Portland

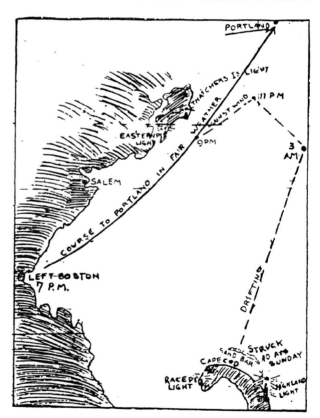

veered off. Captain Cameron observed the Portland rolling and pitching badly. At 11:15 p.m. the captain of a schooner bound for Gloucester saw a paddle-wheel schooner. He thought it was the Portland. The next sighting took place at 11:45 p.m. 14 miles southeast by east of Eastern Point, Gloucester. Captain Pellier of the Edgar Randall saw a paddle-steamer with a badly damaged superstructure. He believed it to be the Portland.

Up to this point there is no disagreement as to where the Portland was located, but from this time onward several theories have evolved to explain her fate.

The perplexing questions of when and where she was destroyed are interesting in part because they would give us an idea how long the humanity on board had to endure the hell aboard ship. Watches later found on several victims had stopped between 9:00 and 10:00. Highly respected watchmakers we have consulted, tell us timepieces from that era were delicate and susceptible to any interruption in the balance wheel. Water, grit or any other foreign substance caused them to cease operating almost immediately. That fact narrows the time of sinking to precisely that hour, but was it Sunday morning or evening?

Edward Rowe Snow believed the Portland had managed to survive the storm for 24 hours, not succumbing until Sunday night. Others have raised doubts that even under the best circumstances the ship didn't have enough fuel to run that long. Technically furnishings could have been used to fire the boilers, but no debris was ever found to indicate that, and damage reported

early on by Captain Pellier corroborates the idea the Portland could not have stayed afloat throughout the day on Sunday.

Most captains at the time stated they believed Blanchard, unable to safely return to any harbor, made a run for deeper water as he had done in similar situations before to eliminate the risk of shoals. Then like now this is common practice. If Blanchard had manuevered the Portland offshore, initially he would have encountered less violent seas. That action would place the Portland much further at sea in the early morning of the 27th and south due to drift. That tactic gives credence to the two theories presented here as to where the Portland sank.

Some historical researchers are convinced the Portland sank far to the north of Cape Cod in deep water north northeast of Scituate. That conviction is based in part on the fact that items from the ship were pulled up by fishing vessels in Massachusetts Bay shortly after the storm. A group called the Historical Maritime Group of New England is one such organization and has been working for the last several years to document the location using side scan sonar and computer generated drift analysis. The Boston Herald carried a story in April, 1989, detailing the findings of that group's work.

If the remains of the Portland are confirmed to be there, it is an important find. However, it may be very difficult to ascertain positive identification since currents and worms destroy wood in a fairly short period of time. Some sceptics will only be convinced if parts are retrieved that can be clearly identified as the Portland's.

The following account has the Portland foundering off Highland Light on Cape Cod. This was told to Fred Freitas, co-author of this book, by his mother and uncles. Freitas's great grandfather Michael Francis Hogan was said to be the last man to see the Portland. Freitas's uncle, Fred Gullage confirmed the story. Gullage said Hogan, his grandfather and constant companion as he was growing up, told him story after story about life at sea and the Portland in particular. Fred Gullage became the historian of the Gullage family. History was his passion. He researched and read widely and could be called on to verify any historical query. Because of the richness of these stories and the mystery surrounding the Portland's disappearance, Freitas has had a life-long interest in the steamer Portland.

In November, 1898, Michael Francis Hogan was captain of the fishing schooner Ruth M. Martin. The Martin was owned by the Fulton Fish Market from New York City. She had been fishing off the coast of New England when Captain Hogan sensed a bad blow coming. All hands were called. The storm sails were set as the Ruth Martin left anchorage and began the dash to safety. During this time the glass on board was falling rapidly which confirmed Hogan's fear. The crew was ordered to batten down the hatches and make more secure the dories. Tubs, mills and other moveable articles not in use were stored below. Hogan also ordered any of the crew not on duty to rest in the forecastle, but they were not to remove their oilskins.

The Ruth M. Martin did not reach safety before the gale struck, she was caught at sea. As the drama unfolded, she was off Cape Cod on the morning of November 27 fighting for her life in the fearsome seas trying to stay clear of the treacherous Peaked Hill Bars, which are off Truro. During

the hellish maelstorm a lull occurred around 9 a.m.. It was during this lull that Hogan saw a large white steamer, which he identified as the Portland. Anxious to save his schooner he ordered a distress flag hung in the rigging to attract the steamer's attention. Patrick Droohan, a crew member, also saw the Portland when he went aloft to rig the distress flag. The storm closed in again and the Portland was lost to view. Captain Hogan was able to beach his schooner near Provincetown and on December 1 she was towed into Provincetown Harbor. The Portland was never seen again.

Miss Lillian Small, daughter of the Boston Chamber of Commerce ship observer, Isaac Morton Small, also saw the Portland from her home near the Highland Light during the lull.

These sightings and the fact that wreckage and bodies were found strewn from Provincetown south along the Cape led people to conclude that the Portland had foundered off Cape Cod. On July 1, 1945, Edward Rowe Snow claimed to have located the Portland. He said that he acted on information given him by Captain Charles Carver of Rockport, Maine. Carver had pulled up a doorknob and other articles from the Portland in his drag nets. He also gave Snow the position where these objects were found. Using Carver's coordinates Snow sent a diver down to find the Portland. According to Snow the Portland lay on the bottom close to a granite schooner the Addie E. Snow. Had the two collided and sunk six miles off Highland Light? Maybe, but the vast amount of wreckage which came ashore around Highland Light, seemed to verify for many that the Portland sank off Highland Light.

Regardless of which theory you believe or what the reason was that caused Captain Blanchard to leave India Wharf, we can conclude that the Portland was on schedule when the storm suddenly intensified. Unable to make headway because of raging seas and ferocious winds, terrified that this great pressure on the paddle-wheel shafts might disable and leave them helpless, and fearful that a turn towards the rocky shore of Gloucester would put his ship in a trough broadside to the wind, Captain Blanchard was compelled to turn the Portland out to sea to try and ride out the storm.

We can only imagine the terror of the passengers and crew on board. The passengers closeted in staterooms, tossed about by unmerciful waves, and terrified by the demonic shrieking of the wind, must have experienced the desperate panic of the hopeless.

Sunday November 27

At approximately 5:45 a.m.with the gale blasting the Cape with over 70 mile an hour winds, Captain Fisher of Race Point Life-Saving Station, Provincetown, wrote in his log, " I heard Steamer blow four whistles distress signal called my crew sent [word unreadable] expected to find Steamer close to station got horse harnessed and beach apparatus ready for a jump telephoned to Keeper of PH Bar [Peaked Hills Bar Life-Saving Station] to have his crew ready for a jump." But nothing was seen.

Surfman John J. Johnson of Race Point Life-Saving Station was on patrol one-half mile east of the station at 7:20 p.m. when he found a life preserver "Portland". This was the first sign of the Portland's fate. Johnson said, " I was bound west toward the station, when I found the first

thing that landed from the steamer. It was a lifebelt and it was one-half mile east of the station. At 7:45 o'clock I found the next seen wreckage, a creamery can, 40-quart I guess. It was right below our station, and nine or ten more of them, all empty and stoppered tightly came on there closely together. Jim Kelly succeeded me on the eastern beat, leaving the station at 8:20 p.m. and at 9:30 he found doors and other light woodwork from the Portland on the shore. When I found the lifebelt the wind was north northeast."

Around 11 p.m. a torrent of wreckage was strewn along the shore. Edwin Tyler of the Race Point Station found doors, electric light bulbs, wash stand tops and other wreckage. His most important find was the upper part of a steamer's cabin. By midnight the beach was littered with debris from the Portland.

Surfman Gideon Bowley of Highland Life-Saving Station found the first body in the surf at

THE BOSTON HERALD — FRIDAY, DECEMBER 2, 1898.

North Truro. Later Captain Daniel Gould of Orleans recovered another body near the mouth of the

p. 64

Nauset River. This scene would be repeated many times in the days ahead. The keeper of the Highland Station E. Worthen wrote in his report for November 28. "At 4 a.m. surfman no. 3 called the keeper and said there was wreckage coming ashore. All hands was called one half going each way along the beach, Keeper with surfmen No.s 1,4,&5, went towards the light when abrest of it found some wreckage, and on looking around saw something up close to the bank on going to it found it to be a man with a lifebelt on plainly marked Steamer Portland, we carried the man along shore until we came to a place whare we could leave him with safety, then sent for an undertaker, there being no coroner within a reasonable distance."

The Portland's end was imagined by Thomas Harrison Eames, author of <u>Steamboat Lore on the Penobscot</u>. He wrote,

photo by permission of Marine Museum of Fall River, Massachusetts.

" It seems probable that the intense smashing she received through the night had weakened her, and finally the pounding of the sea under her guards opened her up and allowed tons of water to rush into the hull, flooding engine and boiler rooms, drowning the men working there, and depriving the ship of her power. The passengers above must have experienced a sense of horrified dismay as the vibration of the engines stopped and the ship swung around broadside to the oncoming seas, lurching sickeningly and settling deeper each moment. The water crashing into the helpless vessel would smash any lifeboats which may have remained, tear off doors, and burst through windows and ports, ripping away the sheathing of the superstructure and washing helpless occupants of staterooms to death in a churning sea.

As she took her final plunge, the superstructure was probably torn away at the main deck and was smashed to kindling wood. Those inside were thrown into the icy water as the wooden deckhouse disintegrated, some being killed outright by falling beams and other debris, others being

p. 65

caught in the wreckage and carried under the surface to drown, while many who had equipped themselves with lifebelts or who succeeded in grasping floating wreckage were benumbed by the frigid water and hammered so unmercifully by the gigantic waves that they soon died."

The tragedy of the Portland did not become apparent to the general public until November 30 because communications had been disrupted by the storm and railroads had been stalled and snowed in. The true extent of the damage slowly became apparent as stories of death and destruction were reported. The fears of the family and friends of those missing turned to grief as the story of the Portland's loss became known.

Wreckage and debris had shown up over the outer Cape from Provincetown to Orleans. How many bodies were actually found? The estimates ranged from 35 to 60. How many passengers and crew were on the Portland when she sailed? The number varied from 150 to 191, for the only passenger list was on board the Portland when she sailed.[22] Where did she sink? Why did she sink?

Jot Small, a life-saver from Provincetown, was asked why so many different opinions about the loss of the Portland and responded so fluently.

"Take my advice," he said. " Don't try to understand it, for that would be impossible. It is just a mystery, and it always will be. There is so much that can't be explained, so many things happened that just couldn't happen, that we are all mystified by the whole affair. What happened to the Portland will always stay a mystery from start to finish. Mark me well!!'

THE BOSTON HERALD.

HERALD CO., Proprietors.   THURSDAY MORNING, DECEMBER 1, 1898.   ...   PRICE TWO CENTS

HER DEATH ROLL
FOREVER A SECRET.

---

[22] Because of the loss of the Portland without an accurate list of passengers, pressure forced steamship companies to keep a duplicate list of passengers at their offices.

The Boston Daily Globe.

IF YOU WANT **RESULTS**
For Your Ad in
The Daily Globe
Largest Circulation in N. E.

BOSTON, WEDNESDAY MORNING, NOVEMBER 30, 1898. TWELVE PAGES. PRICE TWO CENTS.

OVER 125 LIVES LOST

WAITING FOR THE BODY TO COME ASHORE AT ORLEANS

DOCTOR DAVIS EXHIBITING ARTICLES FOUND ON BODIES IN THE HOPE OF SECURING IDENTIFICATION

ALL-DAY SEARCH FOR BODIES FROM PORTLAND

p. 67

PORTLAND'S VICTIMS

Mrs. Horace Pratt & 17 yr. old daughter

Jennie Edmonds

Charles Thompson Wife & Child

Lewis Metcalf

Stewardess Carrie Harris

J.A. Dillon

Cornelia Mitchell

Steward A. Matthews

Harry Smith

J.K. Gately

Hugh Merriam

CHAPTER 12
Scituate Devastated!

"Fannie, Elijah and I went down to Sand Hills yesterday and such a sight- dead men, houses turned bottom side up, others twisted entire around, every house has been changed." Ann Rosini Clapp

Ann Rosini Clapp
photo courtesy of Dorothy Langley,

Once the raging storm waters had subsided, the residents of Scituate began to realize the changes that had been inflicted upon their town by the storm. Ann Rosini Clapp in a letter to her daughter Helen wrote, " There was a woman drowned at the Sand Hills. There is hardly a house standing there. All our tracks are twisted up like sticks - boats loose - barrels all over the meadows. Five men washed ashore at Sand Hills also a pilot boat came way up on those lots of Sam Barker's and there was one dead man in that. - 25 dead bodies washed ashore this side of Plymouth, all North Scituate beach houses are swept away (all the lower ones). Isn't it dreadful a man in a shanty on Stage House Beach was rolled over and over and landed up by Everett Torries." Thursday of the same week the letter continued, " Fannie, Elijah and I went down to Sand Hills yesterday and such a sight- dead men- houses turned bottom side up, others twisted entire around, every house has been changed."

A Boston Herald reporter walked Scituate beaches from North Scituate to the Third Cliff on November 29, 1898. His article was a chronicle of destruction. He found seven bodies and three unknown wrecks. This along with wreckage floating ashore led him to estimate that 100 bodies were floating under the water from Hull to Plymouth. He, like Ann Rosini Clapp, mentioned that one woman had drowned. That person was Mrs. Joseph Wilbur.

Joseph Wilbur and his family were still in their cottage at Sand Hills when the storm struck. As the storm intensified and fearing for their lives, the Wilburs, along with some friends attempted to reach Jonathan Hatch's home. The tide by this time had swept over the beach and filled the pond area behind the beach. Mr. Wilbur and a friend carried Mrs. Wilbur, but they were twice knocked from their feet. A huge wave swept the three of them into Scituate Harbor where Mrs. Wilbur tragically drowned after she had been torn from the grasp of her husband. Her body was later washed up and found in the street. Had the party remained in the cottage at Sand Hills, they would have all perished, for the house was totally destroyed![23]

---

[23] This occurred in almost the exact location on Jericho Road during the Blizzard of 1978 when a child and a DPW worker were thrown from a rescue craft by the raging waters and were drowned.

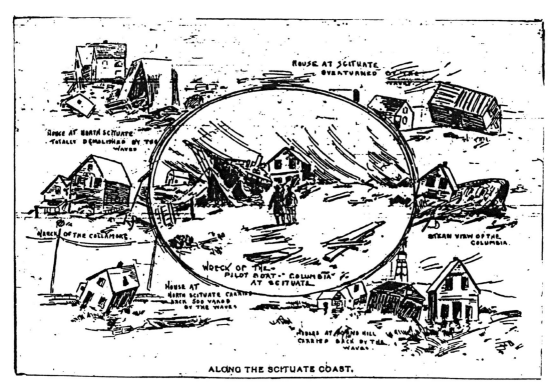

ALONG THE SCITUATE COAST.

Another similar story, but one with different results, also happened in Scituate during the gale. Mr. & Mrs.H.M. White, their daughter and one servant, all from South Braintree, had arrived in Scituate Saturday to spend the weekend at their cottage. During the storm's height on

Note the overturned mossing shanty at Sandhills.

Saturday night and with the tide waters around the building, the wind caused the veranda to be torn off the house.

The frightened family thought they were going to die as the wind and water shook and rocked the house. They were forced to stay in the building until the tide receded. As soon as they could, they left and took refuge in a neighboring home. The continuing storm on Sunday drove them out of that haven to a safer position in the post office.[24] Their cottage, like the Wilbur's, was reduced to rubble. If they had remained, they would have died.

The carnage the reporter detailed was horrible. He started at the extreme north end of North

On left: Mass. Humane Station Minot wrecked. House on the right was Bar Rock Cottage, Minot.

Scituate by describing nine buildings that were swept and blown from their foundations, carried across the pond behind the beach, and deposited in a pasture. The total distance from their original foundations to the pasture was 500 yards. Everett Litchfield's new small cottage was gone with nothing left. His neighbor's home (William Pratt) was twisted off its foundation. The next house in line was knocked off the foundation and pushed into the street. There the waves pounded it to rubble. The story of the destruction went on and on. Even the Mass Humane Life-Saving house was wrecked and their boat damaged.

He moved on to Egypt beach and explained what had happened there. Egypt Road was once a narrow ridge he stated, but now it was a broad, rock-strewn way.

At Sand Hills over 60 cottages were damaged or destroyed including the Mass Humane Society Station # 27 on Jericho Road, the house floated off in one direction, the boat in the other.

---

[24] This might be the post office at Sandhills.

Mass. Humane Station No. 27 Jericho Road, Scituate, before the storm.

In Scituate Harbor buildings were flooded and moved from their foundations. The Harbor along Front Street was under three feet of water. Debris was strewn everywhere. Houses were on their sides, ships forced up on shore and roads under water. The heaviest loss was sustained by George F. Welch, whose lumber and lime wharf suffered severely. Close by this

wharf, and high and dry on Stagehouse Beach, was the lumber schooner Robert Kenner of Bangor. She had dragged her anchors and went ashore, but there was no loss of life and little damage to the vessels.

The loss to mossers was large. Barrels and barrels of moss were swept away- likewise their boats and gear. Thousands of dollars worth of trees were mown down in a day by the gale, and for many months the sounds of saws cutting up these trees was heard throughout Scituate.

Robert Kenner grounded at Stagehouse Beach.
Note Scituate Light in the background.

The bridge leading to First and Second cliff was washed away resulting in $4,000 damage.

South of Greenbush Railroad Station the bridge and tracks were damaged, all traffic below there being diverted by way of Kingston and Whitman for a time.

On the beach at the corner of Gannett & Henry Turner Bailey Causeway.

CHAPTER 13
Wreck and Ruin on the South Shore

" The greatest damage to houses along the shore occured at the Sand Hills in Scituate, at Nantasket Beach and the vicinity of Gun Rock, and at North Scituate Beach. . . . The injury to beaches and shore roads in Cohasset was considerable . . . ."   Oliver H. Howe

---

After the storm winds had abated, a full assessment of the storm's damage began. As communications began to be reestablished, the full extent of the devastation became tragically

Destruction in Hull. Photo courtesy of David Wadsworth.

Destruction in Plymouth. Photo courtesy of Richard Boonisar.

apparent. Newspapers, at first, had treated this storm lightly -- but the disastrous toll to life and property made the headlines grimmer and grimmer as the days followed.

A BLIZZARD IS UPON US

Yesterday was a winter day. The mercury failed to rise above the freezing point . . . . chill easterly wind bore on its breath the promise of an approaching snow storm.

Snow began to fall in Boston, very lightly, about 7:30, and half an hour later gave promise of development into a healthy storm. . . .

The weather bureau was of the opinion the storm would last well into today, and with a continuance of the conditions last described above there was promise of serious trouble at a date almost unheard of in recent years.

(SUNDAY HERALD- NOVEMBER 27, 1898)

GLOBE EXTRA!
5 O'CLOCK
170 VESSELS

Graves in the Vasty Deep for Scores of Seamen All Along the New England Coast, and the Fear is That the List Will

be Monumental-- Lives Lost in This Harbor Are Many--

Trying to Save Craft in Jeopardy.

(THE BOSTON GLOBE, EVENING EDITION NOVEMBER 28, 1898)

MORE DISASTERS.

Awful Story of Wrecks and Loss

of Life Increases Hourly

(BOSTON DAILY ADVERTISER, WEDNESDAY MORNING NOVEMBER 30, 1898)

All along the South Shore the damage from the storm read like a litany of destruction.

p. 75

HULL

When the summer of 1898 wound down, vacationers in Hull left some of the most extensive and beautiful beaches on the South Shore. They certainly didn't think they would make an unplanned visit back the week after Thanksgiving to witness vast devastation, and train operators never expected to see their familar faces again until next summer. How wrong they both were!

UP THE BEACH FROM PEMBERTON TO NANTASKET.

What a sight was awaiting the gawkers flocking to Hull. Their fond memories of the past halcycon summer, of riding the rollercoaster, the ferris wheel, bathing on the beach and the water slide called the chutes, were quickly replaced by the horror of what they saw.

Those standing on Atlantic Hill had a full view of the damage. Hotels built too close to the water's edge had sustained extensive damage-- the same held true for cottages. Between the Chutes and Wade's Hotel (where the Atlantic Bar and Grill is now located on Nantasket Beach), only the

Ferris Wheel and Roller Coaster. Photos courtesy of Richard Cleverly.

Hotel Nantasket had escaped with minor damage. Numerous other hotels had porches, piazzas and decks washed away, and some were badly weakened.

HOTEL NANTASKET.

A long section of track of the Nantasket Line operated by the New York, New Haven & Hartford railroad was badly twisted and undermined, and the electric trolley that ran the length of Hull had sustained serious damage. Before the storm on the Weir River side, four pleasure steamers lay secured to the Nantasket Pier. When the water rose above the pier, the Mayflower, which was the pride of the fleet, was driven up onto the pier and damaged.

p. 78

At every point that was near the tide line the embankment washed away, and at other points the railroad bed was gravely damaged.

Tremendous piles of timber and debris that had been bathhouses, a dance hall, and cottages too numerous to count, lined the entire length of beach. Several structures were washed into Straits Pond. Houses away from the reach of the ocean suffered damage from the wind.

Brunswick And Allerton House

Green Hill in background
The Maguire Cottage
Bottom of Cottage Washed Away

The schooner Leander W. Beebe, 749 gross tons, lay sunk 1/4 mile off the south end of North Beach. Wreckage from her added to the pile of debris on the shore. The plight of her crew of nine was not discovered until after the storm. Nothing could have been done to help them as she was past the reach of the Life-Saving crew. The identity of the ship was not determined until the recovery of the body of her captain.

p. 79

Destruction at Hull. Photo courtesy of Richard Cleverly.

HINGHAM

Great damage was done to the Hingham waterfront. The following diary entries were written by George Lincoln, a well known business man and noted Hingham historian. Lincoln wrote:

"<u>Nov. 27, 1898</u>. A very heavy snowstorm & gale began last night continuing with great

Photo courtesy of David Wadsworth.

violence through the morning, with dark clouds & a high wind in the afternoon. The tide came into the harbor in great rollers, rough & discolored, extending up over the wharves, the streets & meadows. Every boat at her moorings was sunk or driven high up on the beach, & the lumber on Wilder, Kimball's and Whitneys whaves was scattered about the harbor presenting a scene of devastation the like of which has not been seen here since the great gale of April 16, 1851. . . ."

December 1, 1898. "News of the disasters by the Great Gale. . . & loss of life continue to reach us."

December 2, 1898. "Crowds of people go to Nantasket to see the wreckage, dismantled houses and destruction of roads."

December 3, 1898. "The rush to the beach continues. The street cars are doing a great business - crowded front and rear; and only standing room with for late comers."

December 4, 1898. " Great crowds of people at Nantasket Beach. Extra street cars running there as there have been all the past week. It seems as tho' there was no end to the sightseers who seemingly come from all quarters."

Residents of South Shore coastal neighborhoods can easily relate to the last diary entry after having experienced the same huge influx of sightseers after the 1978 and 1991 storms!

COHASSET

In Cohasset the words of Oliver Howe described the havoc. According to Howe, damage was caused by the high wind and the very high tide. "All the woodland, even that situated several miles from the shore, suffered severely. Many pieces of pine woodland had half the trees uprooted. A few trees had their trunks snapped off midway. . . . The uprooting of trees was facilitated by the facts that there was no frost in the ground at the time and that the foliage of the pines was loaded with snow.

"The streets of the town were all impassable because of snow and of branches of trees and whole trees blown down across them to an extent never before seen by the writer. The electric-light poles and wires were sadly disarranged. Many poles were prostrated and the wires were in many instances low or trailing on the ground.

" . . . the most permanent damage was done to Bassing Beach. For many years past this beach has been used by a number of Cohasset men for the purpose of bleaching and drying Irish moss. For the men thus engaged, mossing has furnished a continuous occupation for the summer. The beach before the storm had upon it twenty-two small buildings, most of them being used for the storing of moss, but several served for temporary dwellings of the mossers and two were used as gunning shanties. The storm moved or demolished all these buildings but one, and lowered the beach a good deal, making it less suitable for mossing purposes. . . .

" All of Border Street west of Gulf bridge was under water and was made impassable for horses by being thickly strewn with lumber, fence posts, and other debris, which was in places piled three feet high. Several boats, including one sail-boat, were left in the middle of the road. The level of the water against Tower's building . . . was 33 1/2inches above the street.

View at Cohasset, looking east from Kents Rocks.

Border Street in Cohasset before the storm (top) and after the storm (bottom). Photo courtesy David Wadsworth

"At high tide men were traversing the streets about the Cove in rowboats. . . .

" The water poured through the depression between Atlantic Avenue and Stockbridge Street making an island of all beyond."

NORWELL

Joseph Merritt wrote in his history of Norwell, " In the great storm of November 27, 1898, there was a large amount of heavy growth of white pine uprooted and overturned and for the next five years the local mills and the portable steam mills that were brought in to help, were very busy in working it up, several million feet being marketed."[25]

MARSHFIELD

In Marshfield the eyewitness accounts of Carrie Phillips and Benjamin B. Manter told a tale of danger, destruction, courage and bravery. Carrie Phillips wrote, " . . . will try to give you a little account of how we are left at Brant Rock. I cannot tell you just how many houses are wholly destroyed. . . . but a great many, and nearly all are damaged to some extent. Our large Stetson House was the only one out of our five that was damaged much. Walter P. had four houses nearly destroyed, one barn and his large stable damaged considerably. . . . Edgar Philip's house is gone entirely, and the roof is at my back door. Miller Brigg's house at the corner of Dyke road has sailed over to Cut River. . . . Sea walls are all gone. There is hardly room to drive a team by Churchill's, the bank has washed away so but the hotel was not hurt much or the houses up the street. The roads are full of great rocks and wreckage of all kinds, lobster traps, boats and furniture. I can look out of my window and see a nice bed lounge and stoves, etc., scattered around. Webster Park is a thing of the past; the sand hills are flat. Scarcely a house remains to tell there ever was a settlement there. . . .

"Duxbury Beach is nearly destroyed. A great many houses are destroyed and others badly damaged. In the height of the storm a schooner was driven over the beach into the bay safe. . . .

"I have tried to give you an idea how things are, but I cannot describe things half as bad as they are." In the next part of the letter Carrie tells what she personally experienced. It is a tale told simply, but a tale of courage and bravery. "[Saturday] We did not sleep much for the wind was something terrible. At 8 a.m. Sunday the breakwater gave away and seas broke through on to the street. At 8:30 the street was full of water, and H. said Mr. Bryant's family had gone to the church and I must get the children dressed to go. So the men took Mr. C's three little ones, Mr. Landry's two, and my two little ones to the Church; also Mr. Peterson's two youngest. It was all they could do to get there. Then Leslie Peterson and Henry took me. We had to dodge piazza roofs and boards, for they were flying through the air.

BRANT ROCK
UNION CHAPEL
BUILT C.1895 BY LUTHER WHITE
STONEWORK-FOSTER EWELL
SHELTERED VICTIMS 1898 STORM
EARLY MASS. HUMANE SOCIETY
SHELTERS OR CHARITY HOUSES
STOOD ALONG THE BEACH
1893 LIFE SAVING STATION BUILT
EASTERLY OF THIS SITE.
1915 BECAME U.S. COAST GUARD
STATION CLOSED 1947 RAZED 1967

---

[25] History of South Scituate - Norwell Massachusetts by Joseph Foster Merritt

"I wanted to get to the church where the children and nearly all the women were, but we had to stop at the life saving station and be thankful to get there.

"Just as we landed on the station steps Brigg's house sailed away. We went into the station and I thought I was wet and uncomfortable then but it was nothing compared to what I got later on. We had only been in the station a few minutes when . . . the stones broke the windows of the station towards the beach, and when the big doors gave away, and we women and

Typical storm damage to interior of South Shore homes. Photo courtesy of Richard Cleverly.

children got on to the tables and chairs. Then we thought the station was going, but they ordered the men to break down the doors on the street side to let the water and rocks go through, and that is

what saved us. They did not dare for us to go upstairs. They ran a line over to the church and fastened it to the stone porch thinking we might get over on that, but Mr. Harris, who carried it over, nearly lost his life getting back. The rope slackened up and the rocks knocked his feet from under him and the rope got around his neck. Henry and Baker went to his rescue. So you see what danger there was to get into the street and off your feet. They ran the life boat out and strapped life preservers on to us, even to the little baby.

"When we found there was a chance for the station to stand, and we were drenched through, and the rocks were coming in by cartloads, the men said we better get upstairs. We were glad to get out of waves and rocks. I thought my feet were frozen but I found when we were clothed in some of the clothes supplied by the government for wreckers that we were quite comfortable. . . .

"Now just a word about how the dyke was damaged. In one side of dyke house there was a hole made about 50 feet across. They are trying to repair it. . . .

"There were two wrecks here - one up on the bank by Peace Haven, in which all were saved, and one with 14 men on her, five of whom died from exposure. Further up four Germans lost their lives. None of the residents lost their lives, so we ought to consider ourselves fortunate, I suppose."

Benjamin B. Manter, keeper of the Brant Rock Station, wrote in his report for November 27, " All of the station blankets and pillows and some station wood were taken to the chapel. There were 28 people, including the station crew, who stayed in the chapel through the night. The patrol was not maintained during the night because the crew were so exhausted from the unusual hard work of the day."

In a newspaper article dated December 1 it was stated that a six-foot steering wheel, a spar seventy-five feet long, with rigging attached, and what appeared to be the front quarterdeck house or the side of a steamer's state room was reported floating in the water near Brant Rock. It concluded that people thought it came from some deep-sea ship that wrecked further up the coast.

DUXBURY

"The high tide yesterday carried away one end of the Duxbury pier bridge, and swept away many cottages on the beach, while other structures were more or less damaged. The railroad track walker reports numerous washouts in his section and it is evident that a wrecking train will have to precede the first through passenger train. The fishermen were very fortunate in not losing their craft, although many were sent high up on the land." (Boston Advertiser, November 30, 1898.)

The New York Times reported that a body had been found November 29 on the outside beach near Powder Point Bridge by the Gurnet Life-Saving Crew, clad in oilskins, marked 'Haley' . They mistakenly thought it was one of the men missing from their gunning shanty on the North River.

PLYMOUTH

The storm caused widespread destruction. At high tide Sunday the entire length of Water

Street was afloat with the sea washing completely around Plymouth Rock.

Plymouth Harbor before the storm (top); Plymouth Harbor after the storm (bottom). Photos courtesy of Richard Boonisar.

The bridge at the mouth of Town Brook was floated off its foundation and driven up stream. The roof of a small building was cast into the place where the bridge stood and served as a footway

during the day.

Plymouth beach was badly washed, and of the 141 cottages which once stood there,only two are standing, the others having been smashed and drifted ashore at the head of the harbor in pieces. The baggage room and ticket office at Pilgrim Wharf was a complete wreck, and the wharf itself badly washed through. The Plymouth Yacht Club-house was carried off its site.

Big trees were down in many parts of the town, and on Court Street a big elm branch struck through a roof of a building. Extensive washouts occurred on the railroad, especially the first two miles out from Plymouth. ". . . the belfry of the Town Square Church of the Pilgrimage reposed 190 yards away."

"The fire alarm system was a wreck and there were no electric lights."

The New York Times reported: " it would be a week before telephone wires would give connection to Brockton, where this town connects for Boston, and other places."

(The above information concerning Plymouth, was gleaned from several newspaper accounts written on the days following the storm.)

A lone piano is a grim reminder of the storm's damage. Photo courtesy of Richard Cleverly.

CHAPTER 14

The Aftermath

"When our perils are past, shall our gratitude sleep?" George Canning

Some consequences of the 1898 storm were immediate, others carried on for several years and a few continue to this day. The storm was bad-- very bad. Over 100 vessels and 400 lives were lost in less than 24 hours. This terrible toll of ships and their crews will never happen again because present technology can detect this type of storm, and commercial shipping today obviously is not dependent upon the wind for propulsion and wood for hull construction.

After any major storm, the first question asked is how did the storm compare with past events. Two accounts given here provide the answer. Oliver Howe discussed in Chapter 9, provides important insights in his book, "Cohasset Genealogies and Town History," published in 1909. In that book he states, "A comparison of the height of tide in the two storms [April, 1851, that toppled the first Minot's Light, and 1898] may be of interest. In the "old paint shop" on the wharf near Tower's store there is an old mark with the date 1851 against it showing the height of that great storm. Mr. Edwin Souther has made a mark in the same building for this storm 28 3/4 inches above the floor and 13 inches higher than the mark of 1851."[26] Howe went on to describe how he had copper bolts placed at strategic places around the harbor showing the 1898 tide height. He also referred to the relative good fortune that at the time of the storm there was not a high course of tides running. NOAA records show the predicted morning tide of November 27 was at 10.16 a.m. and 10.3 feet.

Data from the Army Corps of Engineers shows an interesting comparison of five of the regions Great Storms.

Storm Date	Observed Elevation (Boston)	Adjusted Elevation 1992 Sea Level (NGVD)
December 26, 1909	9.90´	10.55´
April 16, 1851	10.10´	10.53´
February 7, 1978	10.40´*	10.52´
November 27, 1898	9.61´**	10.23´
December 29, 1959	9.36´	9.65´

*Note that the 1978 Blizzard produced the highest tide ever recorded.

**Elevations at Cohasset Harbor. NOAA has no data for Nov., 1898 at Boston.

---

[26] The Federal Government kept accurate tide records from 1844-1867 and 1921 to the present. Several government agencies kept records from 1867-1921, but the accuracy for some years is questioned by statisticians.

The week following the storm Frank Wellock, a veteran pilot captain, gave his thoughts to a reporter as to how the Portland Storm compared to the Minot's Light Gale of 1851. Captain Wellock made the following statements to the Boston Advertiser, "There was never anything like it within my experience, and I can remember as far back as the great storm of 1851.

". . . . I never want to have to go through another such experience as had to endure on the pilot boat Minerva from 3 to 5 Sunday morning when the gale was at its height. We were anchored in President's Roads [Outer Boston Harbor], and the strength of our chains and anchors was our salvation.

"I have been out in gales before of course, but none of them are worth speaking of in comparison to this one."

YOU'LL FIND US ROUGH, SIR, BUT YOU'LL FIND US READY

Otis Barker was convinced the remains of the Columbia had economic potential, so he purchased the hulk shortly after the storm. One of his first tasks was to construct an observation deck, fireplace and chimney. All his furnishings had a nautical theme, many being built from extra parts from the ship itself. Barker also was interested in Charles Dickens, and his effort reflected this. A visit inside made a person feel as if he/she had been transported to the home of Dan Peggotty on an English beach. Many of Scituate's youths were the beneficiaries of Barker's unusual work.

In the early 1900's the boat/cottage was assessed by the town at about the same value as adjacent small houses -- $500.00.

The Columbia remained as a tourist attraction until the late 1920's or early 1930's when the rotting structure was removed. Ironically, the mantelpiece is now above the fireplace at the James House, which the Scituate Historical Society is currently transforming into a maritime museum. The James House is located on the Driftway in Scituate.

p. 89

RELATIVES OF THE PORTLAND VICTIMS FILE SUIT

When the Portland Steamship Company learned two of the victims' estates filed suit against them, the company filed a petition with the U.S. District Court in Maine on December 24, 1898. The thrust of this petition was to block these and other filings against the company and to transfer all assets of the Portland to a trustee. The company's assumption that other victims' estates would join the litigation proved correct. By early 1899 at least 55 claims had been submitted to the court.

The compensation sought by the litigants ranged from $5,000 to $10,000. Those seeking $10,000 included $5,000 for bodily injury and $5,000 for mental pain. Small amounts often were added for loss of property ranging from $50 to $300.

Testimony and filings continued through the spring of 1899. The court handed down its decision on May 23, 1899. The Portland Steamship Company was ordered to pay the sum of $10.00 to the trustee! The estates and attorneys of all victims were handed the following decision by the court: "It is further ordered, Adjudged, and Decreed that all other persons whomever, claiming, or who may hereafter claim, for any loss, destruction, damage, or injury. . . .be, and the same hereby are, perpetually restrained and enjoined from bringing, commencing proceedings. . . against the Portland Steamship Company. . . ."

Imagine that kind of decree in today's litigious society. The court's position was that the ship was lost by an act of God. The same type of decision was handed to the victims of the Titanic which sank in 1912. Times were different then.

There is an interesting twist to this story. The Monthly Weather Review, November 1898, published by the U.S. Army Signal Corp. did a little posturing by publishing excerpts from national newspapers castigating Captain Blanchard for sailing in the light of all the warnings.

An interview with an experienced captain and printed in a Boston paper at that time, gives a

different perspective, "Was it not foolhardy for a sidewheeler to go out when such a storm was predicted?

"No. The Signal Service doesn't always hit it right. If the bureau could always be depended on, why it might have been."

His complaint against weather forecasters' accuracy still can be heard today!

The sidewheel method of propulsion for ocean-going vessels in this area was doomed by the fate of the Portland. The new century saw the acceptance of the screw steamer.

NORTH RIVER: AN OLD MOUTH AND A NEW INLET!

Shipbuilders a half century earlier had hoped for a cut to the sea between the third and fourth cliffs because the old mouth was shallow and placed a limit on the size of the vessel that could be navigated seaward. Evidence suggests that some builders in the 1800's had made a clandestine but futile attempt to dig a stream through the barrier, but now it was too late. The industry had faded away after the Civil War because the supply of timber was consumed and the age of sail had given way to steam.

The new cut provided less resistance for the flow of water and the old mouth gradually filled up with sand over the next several years. Salinity levels of the marshes increased which altered the flora environment. Trees growing near what is now called the Spit soon died and the salt haying business ceased within the passage of several years because more coarse grasses took over. The white cedar trees as far west as Job's Landing in Pembroke died. Their spectral skeletons still can be seen west of Route 3 today.

Before the old mouth permanently closed, the Hotel Humarock's guests were treated to a motorboat excursion from the bridge south on the river then east through the old mouth, north along the beach, west through the "new inlet" and back to the hotel.

Today the only hint left of the river's original exit to the sea is a road at that location called Old Mouth Road. Ninety-eight years after that terrible storm the tempest that in a few short hours tore away the connection between Third and Fourth Cliffs is still shown on nautical charts as the "New Inlet"!

"YOU ARE NOT TO GO NEAR THE RIVER-- EVER!"

The family of the Henderson boys never forgot the tragedy that met Fred and Burt Henderson on November 27, 1898. Ray Henderson of Norwell recently told us that the loss of his

Ray Henderson standing
next to Burt & Fred's grave.

uncles has had a lasting affect on the family. Ray's father had a total disinterest in the river that approached a dislike of that body of water. His father never allowed Ray to swim or fish there. Considering the loss the Henderson family suffered, this attitude is understandable.

The loss of the Henderson boys also had another effect upon the people of the town of Norwell. Because the boys were associated with the North River Boat Club, their deaths and the fact that the boat house floor was flooded at every tide interest in the club waned. It seemed that it would not be possible to enjoy sailing because of the changed conditions. The knell was tolled. At a meeting on September 8, 1899, it was decided to sell the Boat House at public auction. It was purchased and moved. On September 16, 1899 the North River Boat Club was dissolved-- another victim of the storm.

Edna Clapp of Scituate would marry Harry Henderson (Fred and Bert's brother) in 1903.

HOME OF THE NORTH RIVER BOAT CLUB
At Union Bridge

p. 92

Boat Club building now on Winter Street in Norwell.

JES SMITH AND FAMILY

Norman Smith in an article from the Maine Mason told the full story of his uncle Jes Smith. He said that he often wondered if Jes and his family were the last people on board that doomed ship. "They had won the race against time to reach the ship- only to keep an untimely rendezvous with Death in the cold, gray Atlantic." He concluded by saying, "But they will never be forgotten, for the bronze plaque that my father, in loving memory, had placed on the headstone of the family plot in Forest City Cemetery had seen to that. It reads:

Jes J. Smith, Age 32

His wife and Two sons

Lost on S/S Portland

Boston to Portland

November 26, 1898

HULL

The residents and businessmen of Hull recognized they still had three tremendous assets hidden beneath the wreckage strewn from one end of the town to the other-- the best beaches on the South Shore, an excellent transportation system from Boston (although damaged) and the desire of people to enjoy these amenities.

In 1905 Paragon Park arose from the rubble. Each successive year new rides and attractions were added, and the new entertainment area bloomed. The 150 foot tower in the middle anchored the park while surrounding it were huge attractions. "The Johnstown Flood of 1889" was one. Another was "Mysterious Asia and the streets of Cairo"-- the dancing girls and sets were imported

p. 93

from Egypt! Gondolas from Italy with their gondoliers crooning songs of Venice ushered visitors around the lagoon. Authenticity was important. The cowboys for the wild west show came from the 101 Ranch in Oklahoma, and the Japanese from the Japanese Village hailed from Tokyo. Even the camels and the camel drivers, who offered camel rides around the park, came from Egypt. In addition, the beautiful floral arrangements and shrubs in the center of the lagoon made this park one of the finest attractions in the world!

FREDERICK FRANZEN OF SCITUATE

Frederick Franzen, who would become the keeper at the North Scituate Life-Saving Station in 1906, was kept very busy during the Portland Gale. At the time of the storm Franzen was surfman # 1 at the High Head Life-Saving Station on Cape Cod, one of the most dreadful spots along the coast. This station was about 5 miles from Provincetown and located between the Peaked Hill Bars Station on the west and the Highland Station on the east. He had been a member of the crew from this station for sixteen years since he joined the Life-Saving service. Prior to this service he had been a boatman, fisherman, coastwise sailor, and whaleman.

Franzen was born on August 19, 1863, in Provincetown. His wife was Catherine Sylvey also of Provincetown. He was described in 1902 as a most experienced life saver, an expert surfman, and a faithful coast guardian.

On November 26 Franzen was home visiting from 6 a.m. until 3 p.m.. After his return to the station, Franzen pulled patrol duty twice-- one, the midnight to 4 a.m. western patrol, and the other, the sunset to 8 p.m. eastern patrol. "He was patrolling his beat on shore, but the sea had cut in through the great sand bastions and Franzen found himself head over heels in the current that was surging in from the sea. He was cast about by the waves until he was thrown high enough on the beach to be able to struggle to the solid ground again." His station was busy the whole day. They rushed their beach apparatus to the wreck of the Albert Butler to assist in that rescue, as well as, patrolling the beach the entire day.

Monday November 28 had Franzen busy again on two 4 hour patrols. It was on this day a fellow surfman from Franzen's station found the first body from the Portland.

For years Franzen was the # 1 surfman at High Head. This position was second only to the keeper in command. This apprenticeship and experience led to his unqualified endorsement by Lieut. Haake, Franzen's inspector, and George Bowley, his District Superintendent, for his appointment as keeper in North Scituate.

Franzen took over the reigns as keeper of the North Scituate station where he remained until his retirement.

Descendants of Franzen still reside in Scituate including Richard Franzen, Arthur Wood-- a Scituate Police officer, Jean Wood-- Arthur's mother, Joanne Savinen and her daughter Lisa.

SURVIVORS

The following are examples of houses that have survived Mother Nature's wrath more than once.

Gunrock Rock, Hull - November, 1898   Gunrock Rock, Hull - November, 1995

179 Turner Road, Scituate - November, 1898.   179 Turner Road, Scituate - November, 1995

A WRECK STORY IN BAMBOO

The following story appeared in the December 1, 1898, issue of the New York Times. Its dateline was Plymouth, Massachusetts, November 30, 1898. "A piece of bamboo which was picked up in the surf here brought a story of death and the loss of the schooner Whitewings of Gloucester in the recent storm. F.E. Thomas found the fragment tossing about in the waves and, securing it, found that it contained a letter. The message was as follows:

'We will be lost- thirteen of us- in fishing schooner Whitewings from Gloucester. Have no bottle to put it in. Everything is gone. We are about to go on a raft. Henry Wilder and Frank Haskins are dead. **If I could only see my wife and darling child again.**

Albert Simmons."

Portland's Victims Being Carried Away by Ocean Currents.

STEAMER PORTLAND.

CHAPTER 15

One Hundred Years Later

"It sounded as if all the hounds of hell were loose that night!" Surfman William Murphy

---

One hundred years have passed since those memorable two days in November when the South Shore of Massachusetts, and in particular Scituate, was forever changed. Time has allowed us the perspective to examine dispassionately the events of those days. However, the people who lived through the events weren't as lucky. As we remember and commemorate the tragedy, courage and heroism shown, it is important to remember that this was a story of real people, who like us, were living

Turner Road, Scituate, MA. November 27,1898 - *Courtesy of Mary Ward*

out their dreams, hopes, and lives.

Today we would like to share new evidence that we have uncovered. Since the original publication of this book in 1995, we have discovered several new primary source documents from those days. The first was a remembrance of growing up in

Damage at North Scituate

North Scituate by Daniel Sylvester. He was born in 1849 and spent his whole life at Minot. His recollection, which was published in 1928 when he was 79, gives insight into the storm and what he observed. The second is from a letter written by Matthew Luce concerning the Pleasant Beach Boat House on the ocean in Cohasset. The Boat House was constructed around 1885 by Cohasset sportsmen interested in hunting and fishing. It was a well-built structure which withstood the assault of the Portland Gale while many other buildings around it were destroyed. The Sherbrooke family has taken a special interest in the preservation of this unique piece of Cohasset history. The third are records from McNamara-Sparrell Funeral Home in Norwell. The Sparrell Funeral Home had been in operation since the early 1800's. These three sources give us a deeper feeling for the events of November 26-27, 1898.

First Daniel Sylvester:

> "The storm of November 1898, - I was aroused by the [surfman], that my stable door had blown off. That was at 4 a.m. I got up dressed, and with his assistance, repaired it. It was a terrific gale. The water was running thru past the house two hours before high tide, and the marsh stood three feet under water. The horses in the stable were standing in two feet of water. Eight houses were smashed, or carried away during that time. The town has bought back seventy five feet, twenty five feet each time to preserve and to make new roadways on account of the washing away of the breakwater. A breakwater of plank was first built, jetties were

p. 99

built out into the ocean to check it, but everything failed until the present concrete breakwater was built."

The second account comes from a letter written by a Cohasset resident after surveying the damage along what is now Jerusalem Road. This letter was given to us by Ross Sherbrooke.

"Last Sunday Nov. 26th, was the day of the big storm, the storm which was fiercer by far than the great storm of 40 years ago in which Minot's light was destroyed. We have spent the morning in going along the shore and looking at the frightful havoc which is evident at every step one takes.

The Boat House Cohasset, Ma.

To begin with, the boat house, our staunch old friend, braved the storm nobly and almost unscathed. I don't believe another house along the coast, situated as close to the water's edge as the Boat house is, has withstood the storm. Its fine and massive chimney seems to have been its mainstay. I like to think that a protecting hand sheltered the house of friendship and of hospitality and preserved it alone from the ruthless fury of the elements. The tide rose 10 or 12 twelve feet above its usual height even before high–tide and the whole road between Aldrich's house and Kimball's Hotel was several feet under water, I ought to say under furious waves, and today hardly a vestige of the road remains. Mrs. Roach's house was lifted bodily 12 feet from its foundation; the beach projected itself with all its refuse and rocks in one mass over the road and swept everything in its course along into the still water; not a bathing house is left on the beach and some were carried as far as Hollingsworth's lawn. But the most impressive feature is the wreckage along the whole shore, the silent testimony of the tremendous loss of life. The beach is literally covered with huge masses of timber, masts, spars, and even whole sides of barges.

Our schooner, the Juniata, which we have just visited, was lifted bodily over the Williams breakwater and landed within 50 feet of Mr. Sheldon's house. The crew of 18 men were lashed to the rigging and all escaped unharmed, landing on the breakwater. It was a marvelous escape. Not every ship was as fortunate. Near Green Hill the tops of the masts of a ship protrudes from the water and the bodies of men can be seen at low water

p. 100

lashed to the rigging. Mr. Luce's house had merely a chimney blown down. Mr Faxon's house had its eastern veranda blown over the house and deposited on the front lawn after having knocked down a chimney in its flight. Billy Dean's shanty was knocked all to pieces and his boat was landed in the woods beyond. Johnson and his wife had to leave their house about 10 A.M. on Sunday and Johnson watched the storm from the top of the hill. He said that the Boat house looked from Spaulding's House like Minot's Light in a big storm with the mist dashing clear over it.

The wreckage along the Nantasket beach and Green Hill is frightful, and at Nantasket at least it seems as if things would never fall into their former shape again and everything would be rebuilt differently now that nature has swept away all the eyesores and nuisances. The book of photographs of the wreckage is in the boat house and gives a very graphic picture.

The Portland went down before this same storm, leaving Boston for Portland with a large passenger list and was never heard from again, its wreckage being scattered along the South Shore as far as the Cape, some of it coming ashore near Eastham, at 'My House'. Mat was at My House during the storm,–he started the following afternoon to drive home and he had a lively time of it, arriving at home after the family had gone to bed.–The snow in Boston and suburbs was most remarkable and I have now doubt that this storm surpasses the violence and duration any other storm which has occurred and will during our lifetime.– A.L.K.V."

Mr. Robert McNamara, owner of McNamara-Sparrell Funeral Homes, in Norwell, MA, recently placed on loan with the Scituate Historical Society, their funeral records from 1887 to 1900. These records are an invaluable source to genealogists, but also clearly show the tremendous impact the storm had on the local citizenry.

For a few days after the storm, roads to the beaches were impassable, so a cottage near the wrecked Pilot Boat Columbia was used as a temporary morgue. When the bodies of the crew from the pilot boat were recovered, they were laid out in the living room. In the early 1970's a very elderly man visited the house and recalled helping his father bring in the bodies. What impressed him just as much as the gruesome task of moving the victims, was the cottage's unusual staircase. On his visit over seventy years later, he was pleased to see the stairway was still there. The funeral home records corroborate the fact that the bodies were not immediately picked up.

The bodies of Harry Petersen, Edward Paterson, and Andrew Elligsen were sent to Boston by train for burial elsewhere and Malinda Wilbur's body was transported to Raynham, MA. Three unidentified drowning victims were also found and buried in Scituate. Possibly they were from the pilot boat. However, it is just as possible they were from the schooner barge Delaware or some other vessel.

The deaths of the young men, who drowned in the North River marshes, brought tremendous anguish to all that knew them. There was a private funeral for George Ford in Marshfield on November 30th. Because Fred Henderson, Bert Tilden, and Bert Henderson were close friends, it was decided to hold a triple funeral for them on Saturday, December 3rd. The funeral home record reads:

> "- - - triple funeral in the church. Procession formed with Bert in my hearse. Fred in my small hearse and Bert Tilden in Marshfield's hearse. Met by Phoenix F & A.M. of which this one was a member [Bert Henderson] and escorted to church. Church was full. Masonic service at grave."

It was a service those in attendance never forgot and never wished to witness again. Said a young man speaking of their fate, " It is hard on us who had been associated with them often in labor and in sport.We knew them as others could not because of this intimacy." He continued by saying that the boys were so companionable. They won and retained the esteem and love of others through their conversation and deportment. "All who knew them will be deeply affected. They can never be forgotten."

Reverend T. Thompson, minister of the First Parish Church, in his eulogy said,

> "Besides being industrious and companionable they possessed that measure of honesty and truthfulness that properly goes along with these qualities and so were a type of young men who might have reasonably been expected to take honorable places in conducting the affairs of this town. Considered from these standpoints their death is an irreparable loss to this place. We cannot even afford to have such young men leave us for the better opportunities of the earthly life. We need them and they have been taken from us, and while we must submit, we can but lament their taking off.
>
> They were also young men of skill and bravery which would have been sufficient to have extricated them from many a peril such as would appall others. But it seems certain that no amount of skill could have saved them in the desperate situation in which they found themselves upon that terrible day when wind and wave combined and stout ships went down with all aboard.
>
> I am not satisfied to say of the loss we have suffered, "It was to be," or "It is all for the best." I submit, when I must to calamities such as this, or even of lesser moment. To so acquiesce may easily become an excuse for little thought and may prevent future precautions that at another time might avail. Let us but say, "It was to be," but rather, "It shall not again be."

At least for them it never did. It wasn't until the Great Blizzard of 1978 that such tragedy would again revisit the South Shore.

CHAPTER 16
Steamer Portland Found!
"I once was lost and proud and now I am found and humble. I prefer that other". Dylan Thomas

One hundred and ten years have now passed since one of the most powerful storms to ever strike New England blasted the region. No one is still living that can recall the events of that awful storm, but new discoveries have been made. Edward Rowe Snow, the renowned New England maritime historian, was particularly fascinated by the loss of the Steamer Portland. He spent many years trying

Edward Rowe Snow, Courtesy of Jeremy D'Entremont

to unravel exactly what happened to the ship. The most nagging question for him was where the ship actually sank. Today we know. However, other questions remain unanswered such as when did the Portland sink. Was it 9:30 a.m. on November 27 or 9:30 p.m. that evening? For the sake of all on board the doomed ship we hope it was sooner rather than later. It is unlikely that question can ever be answered. And then there is the question of what exactly happened to the ship. New evidence indicates the Portland met a violent end when her superstructure was swept away, but her upright position on the bottom of Stellwagen Bank is somewhat of a mystery. Researchers from the Stellwagen Bank National Marine Sanctuary continue to explore the wreck site. Most likely they will eventually find the answer to that question and others in the future.

Evidence of the destruction left by this great storm has slowly disappeared, but it can still be observed in such places as the North River marshes. There one can still see stumps of trees that grew there prior to the creation of the New Inlet. Immediately after the storm, salt water flooded these marshes at every high tide and the trees quickly died. The most dramatic evidence of the storm of course is found at Humarock. The storm that cut off Humarock from the rest of Scituate still affects Humarock residents today. The only way to access Humarock today is to cross either the Julian Street Bridge or the Sea Street Bridge. In recognition of the excellent lifesaving work done by Station Keeper Frederick Stanley; a new bridge will replace the old Sea Street Bridge. The new bridge will be known as the Frederick Stanley Bridge and will have a bronze plaque honoring this man-certainly a fitting tribute. This bridge is presently under construction.

PORTLAND LOCATED

Side scan sonar was used to locate and image the *Portland*. Courtesy of Klein Associates Inc.

For over 100 years the location of where the steamer Portland lay buried remained one of New England's greatest unsolved stories, but no longer; the mystery has been resolved. In 1989 Arnold Carr and John Fish located what they believed to be the Portland wreck site, but they were unable to provide clear photographic evidence to validate their claim. That clear photographic evidence would be provided in 2002 by the Stellwagen Bank National Marine Sanctuary and the National Undersea Research Center at the University of Connecticut.

Since 2002 the combined efforts of these groups has led to further conclusive photographic evidence that this is truly the site of the Portland. Because of their extensive

research and the Portland's importance to New England history, the site of the Portland has been added to the National Register of Historic Places.

Archaeologists used the remotely operated vehicle (ROV) *Hela,* to explore the *Portland* shipwreck. Courtesy of NOAA/SBNMS .

Blending new technology, scientific methods, and good old hard work, this joint effort has unearthed historic artifacts like the dishes and the walking beam engine. This tantalizing evidence continues to add to the

A mug lies amongst twisted pipes on the *Portland* main deck. Courtesy of NOAA/SBNMS, NURC-UConn, and the Science Channel.

picture of what happened on those fateful nights of November 26 and 27, 1898. When this evidence is combined with artifacts known to have come from the Portland, like the serving dish that is located at the Maritime and Irish Mossing Museum in Scituate, a more complete picture of the Portland story is unveiled.

Dishware in the *Portland* galley. Courtesy of NOAA/SBNMS, NURC-UConn, and The Science Channel.

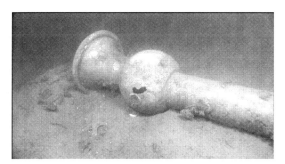

One of the *Portland* steam escape pipes lies on the seafloor east of the shipwreck. Courtesy of NOAA/SBNMS, NURC-UConn, and The Science Channel.

The R/V *Connecticut,* operated by the University of Connecticut, supported the research expeditions to the shipweck. Courtesy of NOAA/SBNMS, NURC-UConn, and The Science Channel.

The Maritime & Irish Mossing Museum in Scituate, owned and operated by the Scituate

Historical Society, has an extensive exhibit on the Portland Gale of 1898.

Emblem on vegetable dish at the Maritime and Irish Mossing
Museum. Courtesy of The Maritime & Irish Mossing Museum.

BIBLIOGRAPHY

BOOKS

Dalton, J.W. The Life Savers of Cape Cod. Sandwich: J.W. Dalton, 1902.

Davenport, George Lyman, and Davenport, Elizabeth Osgood. The Genealogies of the Families of Cohasset
        Massachusetts. Boston: Stanhope Press, 1909.

Fish, John Perry. Unfinished Voyages: A Chronology of Shipwrecks in the Northeastern United
        States. Orleans: Lower Cape Publishing, 1989.

Merritt, Joseph Foster. Old Time Anecdotes of the North River and the South Shore. Rockland: Rockland Standard
        Publishing Company, 1928.

Murphy, Barbara. Irish Mossers and Scituate Harbour Village. Barbara Murphy, 1980.

Murphy, Barbara. Scituate: The Coming of Age of a Plymouth Colony Town. Barbara Murphy, 1980.

Old Scituate. Published by the Daughters of the American Revolution, Chief Justice Cushing Chapter, 1921.

Richardson, John M. Steamboat Lore of the Penobscot. Augusta: Kennebec Journal Print Shop, 1941.

Snow, Edward Rowe. Great Storms and Famous Shipwrecks of the New England Coast. Boston: Yankee
        Publishing Company, 1943.

Snow, Edward Rowe. Storms and Shipwrecks of New England. Boston: Yankee Publishing Company, 1943.

Snow, Edward Rowe. True Tales of Terrible Shipwrecks. London: Alvin Redman. 1963.

Watson, Benjamin (editor). New England's Disastrous Weather. Camden: Yankee Books, 1990.

Whittier, Bob. Paddle Wheel Steamers and their Giant Engines. Duxbury: Seamaster, Inc., 1987.

MAGAZINES

Pappas, Chris. "The Portland Comes Home." **Portland Monthly**. July/August 1989, 10-13, 75.

Seligson, Susan V. "How They Found the Portland." **Yankee**, December, 1989, 68-75, 120-125.

NEWSPAPERS

The Boston Daily Globe. November - December, 1898.

The Boston Daily Advertiser. November - December, 1898.

The Boston Post. November - December, 1898.

The Boston Herald. November - December, 1898.

The Quincy Daily Ledger. November - December, 1898.

The Hingham Journal. December 2, 1898.

The Hull Beacon, November - December, 1898

PHOTOGRAPHIC IMAGES

Stellwagen Bank National Marine Sanctuary.

National Undersea Research Center at the University of Connecticut.

The Science Channel.

Klein Associates, Inc.

Maritime and Irish Mossing Museum, Scituate, Massachusetts.

Jeremy D'Entremont

Printed in the United States
202742BV00004B/251-354/P

9 780981 572062